W9-BZN-740

PENGUIN BOOKS

IN THE DUTCH MOUNTAINS

Cees Nooteboom is the author of five novels, seven volumes of poetry, a play, and several travel books. *Rituals*, his first novel to appear in this country, was awarded the 1982 Pegasus Prize for Literature. Nooteboom lives in Amsterdam but spends part of each year on the island of Minorca, off the Mediterranean coast of Spain.

Adrienne Dixon has translated several novels and short stories from the Dutch and Flemish. In 1974, she received the Martinus Nijhoff Prize for Translations.

IN the DUTCH MOUNTAINS

A NOVEL BY
Cees Nooteboom

TRANSLATED FROM THE DUTCH
BY Adrienne Dixon

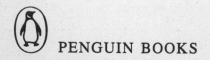

PENGUIN BOOKS

PENGUIN BOOKS
Published by the Penguin Group
Viking Penguin, a division of Penguin Books USA Inc.,
375 Hudson Street, New York, New York 10014, U.S.A.
Penguin Books Ltd, 27 Wrights Lane, London W8 5TZ, England
Penguin Books Australia Ltd, Ringwood, Victoria, Australia
Penguin Books Canada Ltd, 10 Alcorn Avenue, Suite 300,
Toronto, Ontario, Canada M4V 3B2
Penguin Books (N.Z.) Ltd, 182–190 Wairau Road, Auckland 10, New Zealand

Penguin Books Ltd, Registered Offices:
Harmondsworth, Middlesex, England

First published in the Netherlands
by Uitgeverij De Arbeiderspers, 1984
First published in the United States of America
by Louisiana State University Press, 1987
Published in Penguin Books 1991

10 9 8 7 6 5 4 3 2 1

PUBLISHER'S NOTE
This is a work of fiction. Names, characters, places, and incidents
either are the product of the author's imagination or are used
fictitiously, and any resemblance to actual persons, living or
dead, events, or locales is entirely coincidental.

THE LIBRARY OF CONGRESS HAS CATALOGUED THE HARDCOVER AS FOLLOWS:
Nooteboom, Cees, 1933–
In the Dutch mountains.
Translations of: In Nederland.
I. Title.
PT5881.24.O55I513   1987
839.3'1364   87-3289
ISBN 0-8071-1425-1 (hc.)
ISBN 0 14 01.1829 2 (pbk.)

Printed in the United States of America

"Where did we get the story from?"
"Out of the dustbin, with all that old rubbish."

—Hans Christian Andersen

In the Dutch Mountains

1

ONCE upon a time there was a time that some people say is still going on. The Netherlands then were much larger than they are now. Others deny this, and still others say that although such a time did once exist, it does no longer. I don't know which of these views is correct. Yet I have seen the Dutch flag flying from the highest passes in Europe. The North of the country was always around Dokkum, Roodeschool and Pieterburen, but the southern border was several days' drive from Amsterdam or the Hague.

I am a foreigner, but I still remember it all, and I don't intend to keep quiet about it. My name is Alfonso Tiburón de Mendoza. I am Inspector of Roads in the province of Zaragoza, part of the ancient kingdom of Aragón, in Spain. In my spare time I write books. As a student I spent some years in Delft, on a scholarship to study road and bridge building, and I might as well say at once that the northern Netherlands have always inspired me with Fear, a fear that demands a capital letter, German style, as if it were one of the basic elements of which all life on earth is composed, like Water and Fire in the teachings of the early natural philosophers. Associated with this capital letter there is a feeling of being enclosed within a black cylinder, from which there is no easy escape.

Exactly what gave me this feeling I do not know, but it had to do with both the landscape and the people. The northern landscape, like the desert, suggests absolutism. Except that in this case the desert is green and filled with water. There are no allurements, roundnesses, curves. The land is flat, exposing the people, and this total visibility is reflected in their behavior.

Dutch people do not merely meet; they confront each other. They bore their luminous eyes into another person's and weigh his soul. There are no hiding places. Not even their homes can be described as such. They leave their curtains open and regard this as a virtue. I had taken the trouble to learn their strange language, which consists largely of harsh sounds for which the upper area of the throat is used a great deal. I think this must be the result of the inclement conditions, such as breached dykes, east winds and pack ice, which plagued them in the past.

I soon discovered that they regarded it as craven flattery for a foreigner to speak their language and preferred to converse with me in yet another, third language. I have never quite understood the reason for this, but assume it is to do with a mixture of embarrassment and indifference.

Whatever the reasons, I have never felt much at home in the North of their country; on the contrary, I always began to revive only on my way home or when, driving through the Rhine valley, I perceived in the distance the first faint, blue outlines of the mountains separating the cool, flat north from the wilder regions the Dutch call the southern Netherlands. For although I could barely understand the dialects that are spoken south of the High

Passes, and the darker, smaller people living there did not resemble their more enlightened compatriots from the North, I felt at home. Life in the South was less regulated and restricted, and although the central government of the Union obviously tried to keep a tight control, it was only partly successful, owing to the great distances, the independent character of the inhabitants, and their natural dislike of their rulers. In the North they were regarded as second-class citizens, at times openly mocked for their accent, and usually considered fit only for the more menial jobs, which in view of their poverty they had no choice but to accept. These things rankle.

Conversely, most northerners—not counting a few artists—felt equally unhappy in the far South. The civil servants there sought one another's company, talked of the "Dark South," of barbarians and corruption, of a stupid and ungovernable rabble. Accustomed as they were to their own suffocating overpopulation and the resulting necessary social controls, they felt lonely and, in their hearts, afraid. The central administration in The Hague, the national government, was not always able, so they said, to guarantee their safety; some areas, it was alleged, were ruled by gangs, and extortion was rife. Moreover, the South produced nothing but cheap wine and fruit, and only cost the state money. In fact, it served no useful purpose except to provide cheap labor to the northern industrial cities, where the southerners promptly congregated in the former slum areas and were grudgingly tolerated by the locals, until an economic depression led to cries for them all to be sent back, with their smells and their noise, to the primitive place from which they had come. All the same, the national government kept a sharp eye on the rising separatist movement.

2

I FOR one loved the South. It may be something to do with the country I myself come from, although the landscapes of the southern Netherlands do not resemble my part of Spain, which has from time immemorial been called Aragón. The South is darker, full of hidden caverns, like an old engraving printed with too much ink. There are seething rivers and immense, sombre forests. Unlike the North, Aragón is not flat, though it is wide and open, sometimes almost luminous. The green, smug, domesticated landscapes of the North aroused in me a disconsolate boredom equalled only by the aversion I felt for most of the inhabitants, on account of their complacency and their unbridled greed, and the hypocrisy with which they tried to conceal both.

The people of the South were rougher but also freer, just as their landscapes were more rugged and desolate. What repelled others attracted me. The southern plateau was my favorite landscape. Lazy journalists always called it a moon landscape, but I have yet to hear of a moon on which you can sleep in a shelter built of rough boulders beside a rushing mountain stream. Traveling was primitive but adventurous, and the local officials knew enough Dutch for you to make yourself understood. The northerners you met were always complaining that the bread wasn't white enough, the post offices were dirty, television reception was poor—as if those were reasons to be sorry. Their complaints did not end there by any means: too many programs were in dialect, the local police were corrupt, the news from the North didn't seem to interest the southerners, and many town mayors could not be bothered to hang the queen's portrait on the wall. The numbskulls talked of *mare* when they meant the sea, called their border guards *wacchers* and put their toddlers in *walkebandes*; but these words were beginning to die out at the time in which this story is set, not so much because they were deliberately suppressed by the central administration but through the influence of radio and television.

The only people that seemed to regret this were a few poets from the North who believed that in such words and expressions the soul of language itself was preserved; but, as usual, no one else cared. Among themselves, the southerners continued to use these words, though a certain false shame inhibited them from doing so in front of northerners. As a result, relations between the two groups were always somewhat artificial, and of course there was no question of any real national unity. The country was called the Kingdom of the Netherlands, but the people who lived in the mountains, in poverty, and had never seen the sea, could not imagine what feelings they should associate with these words.

The northerners, who never stopped grumbling about the total lack of organization in the South, complained at

5

the same time of the organized crime that made any effective government impossible. The members of parliament representing the South were "all of them bribed and in the service of sinister factions"; and although it can't be denied that in the inhospitable southern regions things happened that could not bear the glaring light of the North, I still loved that recalcitrant, unkempt land with all my heart, if only because there I did not feel stifled by the climate of Good Intentions that makes the polders so insufferable. I suppose I have my Spanish origins to thank for that.

The end of the world would arrive there later and, I was convinced, not with a whimper. I am not by nature a frivolous person, but it seemed to me that in the tame human zoo north of the mountains something had gone irreparably wrong. People who are trying to keep too tight a control over their lives suffer from a false longing for immortality, and no good has ever come of that.

3

THE story I wish to tell happened not so very long ago, and a strange story it is. I tell my stories chiefly to myself, and I think that my other work, with which I earn my living, has helped me to do so. There is a similarity between writing stories and building roads: you are bound to arrive somewhere some time. This idea occurred to me one day near Aguerón, on the C 221 leading from Calatayud to Cariñena. My staff complain that this is the most frequently inspected road in Spain, and there is a mote of truth in that, as they would say in the South, although there is one road I love even more. But the idea came to me on the C 221, and the similarities are nowhere clearer. The road runs over high ground, and the world stretches away on either side; you can take a general view, which is what a writer should do. Gigantic metal pylons, linked by five or six enormous cables, make it seem as though they hold the world, or the story, together. Road signs announce the approach of a spring—a pause for the reader—or a dip in the road or some other hazard. At such points the reader had better watch out.

The writer must not let him swerve off the road, though I know there are writers who aim to do exactly that. Perhaps I have seen too many accidents to be one of them.

I am in my early sixties, fairly stout, and usually good humored. My only peculiarity, apart from writing, is that I always dress in blue. But this is of no importance, I am aware of that. So I won't say any more about myself. I can read a landscape like a book, that is really all I wanted to say. Perhaps it is to do with the so-called omnipotence of writers, their ability to build a world exactly as they please.

In a real landscape this had already happened. About halfway along the C 221, for instance, there lies, to the left of the road, fairly far down, the rectangular shape of a cemetery cut into the dry red soil. There is something irrevocable about it: you, as a traveler, have no choice but to accept it, this patch reserved for death.

Something similar, I think, also happens to the reader. A book is a document and into this document the word *death* is suddenly introduced, though you can, of course, have any thoughts you like about that. But let me get on with my story. It has many bends, like most of the roads in Aragón; sometimes you have to climb and therefore, at other times, descend, for there is not much I can do about the rise and fall of the land—that does not come within my competence, unlike the road surfaces and the verges. If the authorities had their way, the roadsides would be cut regularly by scythe—along the minor roads we still use the scythe—but here and there, in places I myself indicate, I always give orders to leave as many flowers as possible. It is not a very important road, no government ministers pass this way, and who is to inspect the Inspector?

To the point. These meanderings of mine are not without their usefulness. I have already said where my story is set, and that was complicated enough because so few people know the place. That isn't my fault, though. But the theme—perfect beauty and perfect happiness—is not one that I think many of my famous colleagues would write about. And yet this is what my story is about. It begins and ends with it, at least I think so now. You see, as I am about to begin, I suddenly see a stretch of the C 221 before me again, fairly straight, near Nuestra Señora de las Viñas. The plain, the silver olive trees, light patches in the soil as if here too a war had been fought, as at Verdun, and of course so there has. Those patches are there to remind us of evil.

A man on a mule approaches. Rush baskets, earthenware vessels on either side, a dog. Maybe he has been on the road for a whole day, an apparition from paradise, and that was what the main characters in my story were also. Not were, are. But when the story began they lived in Bijlmer, a new suburb of tall apartment blocks on the southern outskirts of Amsterdam. And their names were Kai and Lucia.

How do you introduce the notion of perfect happiness? Don't be tiresome; the asphalt is hot and wet. Put the roller over it! Kai and Lucia were perfectly happy.

Now someone will say that there can be no such thing as perfect happiness among people who have the prospect of old age, sickness and death before them, but you can also turn this the other way around. Someone who does not allow himself to be troubled by this prospect is well on the way toward perfect happiness. I know that this concept is not popular and does not fit in with the image of our time, but that can't be helped. It was simply the truth. Perfect happiness, like perfect unhappiness and anything approaching it, is terrible to contemplate. And besides: far though it be from me to say that perfect happiness cannot exist among ugly people, it has to be admitted that logically there must be a graduated scale, according to which perfect happiness is even more insufferable among perfectly beautiful people than anywhere else. This was the case with Kai and Lucia. They were, as they say in the South, *blamelees*—no one could speak any blame of them; in short, from an aesthetic point of view they were irreproachable. The only thing that could conceivably be rejected, after one look at these two, as indeed it frequently was, was the idea of the aesthetic itself.

People may be beautiful, but when there is absolutely no fault to be found, when one is halted in one's tracks as if thunderstruck when meeting them in the street, then perfect beauty becomes a yardstick by which one measures one's own imperfections, and nobody likes that.

4

As we have been formed by the conventions of European literary culture, there is little scope for an individual writer to exercise his imagination; the terminology has been fixed ever since writing began. Lucia's hair was, of course, golden. (Like *honyseime,* the fat of the honey, as someone in the South was to say later.) She had clear blue eyes like a summer sky, her lips were red as cherries, her teeth white as milk. Anyone trying to think of other words is mad. Culture is a code. Unhappy is the land where no peaches exist, for its people would not know how to describe Lucia's skin. Any other comparison would be inadequate because it would lack the suggestion of eating. The sight of Lucia's skin aroused in everyone, men and women alike, the secret cannibal who lurks in the swampy prehistoric soil of our souls. The proportions of her body were in perfect harmony, according to a golden rule that had thereby become its own touchstone. A Persian poet once called women's breasts the "moons of paradise." This raises the question whether different forms of perfection exist, for the image reminds me more of the seductive sculptures on Indian temples than of the Venus de Milo, who is no more than their shadow. Yet it is better to stay closer to the latter—too much lust seems incompatible with the idea of perfection. Perhaps we should, since we are dealing with an idea, look to the abstractions of artists like Alberti and Leonardo, who have constructed the human body on intersecting lines. I refer to Leonardo's famous drawing of a man who seems nailed to a cross (of beauty) while his feet and arms fan out in many other poses around him. The deification of the body, at the same time nature and concept, the *blamelees* body beside which every living body was bound to be found wanting, even if only out of self-preservation—of course this is insufferable.

Because of my work I am used to certain forms of perfection. Part of my work is based on mathematics, the advanced study of which allows one to discover the loftiness of great poetry without its unpredictable and, let us be honest, its murkily human aspect. On the other hand, we are not speaking here of formulas but of two living beings, whom I am trying to describe here in my classroom in Zaragoza.

It is, I feel the need to say this, the only luxury of my existence. I always spend my holidays on my own, far from my family, in order to write, a folly for which, as I grow older, I am more easily forgiven because the people around me are not so very interested in my odd personality.

My brother is head of a primary school in a suburb of Zaragoza, and during the month of August, when the entire city is deserted because of the extreme heat, the school is at my disposal. I admit it is a little ridiculous, but nobody bothers me and I do not bother anyone either.

My books, if you wish to call them that, are put out by a small publishing house in León—the capital of Asturias—certainly not in my own province. My wife and sons never read them, and what little comment they have elicited has been printed in the smallest type in Spanish provincial papers. This suits me very well. Anything more would only create obligations which, in my description of Kai, to mention the first thing that occurs to me, I can well do without.

I often wonder how other writers—for I am undoubtedly a writer—can keep going after good or bad reviews. But let us go back to Kai. If a computer existed in the form of a scientist who was told to calculate and execute the perfect complement to the female body, the result would be Kai. Sometimes, when Kai and Lucia walked side by side or, less visibly to others, when they lay in bed beside, under or on top of one another, they resembled a living sculpture on which a scholar with Renaissance preferences could have demonstrated to a class of eager students, if such a thing exists, the lines of perfection running from one to the other. For this is the strange thing: they simply could not do anything incongruous. Whatever pose they adopted, however they positioned themselves jointly or separately and with whatever point of contact, their beauty was invariably enhanced. There must exist a law for this, which I am unable to formulate. In brief, and I hope this is almost the last time I shall use the word, they were perfect also as a couple, even when they were a hundred or more meters away from each other, which is not without significance in this story, if only because it aroused an impossible desire, and therefore jealousy.

Kai was muscled like those two bronze statues that, in

the seventies of this almost bygone century, were dragged up from the bottom of the sea off Riace in Calabria, by someone who must have thought he had gone mad. For imagine: you are swimming under water among the seaweed and the strange fishes in the silence of the deaf that reigns there, and suddenly you see, right in front of you, reclining on the already so fantastical sea floor, in a shaft of sparkling light as in old popular prints, two huge male figures, too large to be human, two perfect corpses of an extinct race, mysteriously preserved, asleep on the seabed. The diver rose to the surface where the air bubble of the world burst open, told of his dream vision, and the statues were hauled up, the most beautiful human images ever made.

Everyone knows the gruesome photographs of body builders injected with hormones—shiny knots of muscles like a strange, bulbous form of cancer fixed externally to the human body, a parody of the perfection the gods had once devised for themselves. Exactly on the indefinable borderline between that idea and its twentieth-century excess, Kai's body had ceased to develop further, because it knew that thereafter would begin the vulgarity that results from the exaggeration of the physical, which makes even ordinary beautiful people so boring. Only the artist knows the true standard of perfection, even though he uses it solely as a model against which to measure himself through negation and distortion. Kai's eyes had that not quite describable color halfway between slate and northern seawater, hard but at the same time flowing and gleaming. If Lucia's hair was as blonde as golden wheat, his had since the Middle Ages had the color of raven's feathers, so black that the eye could detect a purple sheen in it.

14

Had they not both possessed an innate innocence, or perhaps a naïve timidity, the admiring gaze of passers-by would long ago have made them vain and coquettish, or worse, turned them into *kitsch,* but they were so engrossed in each other that they scarcely noticed the reactions of others, neither the breathless admiration and longing nor the jealousy and its nocturnal companion, hate.

They had first met in the circus where their parents worked, Kai's father as a horseman, Lucia's parents as trapeze artistes. They had known at once that they could not escape from each other, that their love was fatal, eternal, and that they could never be separated. They need never look for another, because the only possible other had already appeared, namely—though the sentence may now be ungrammatical—they themselves.

5

THE idea of perfect beauty also suggests the thought of other abstract qualities. However, fate had treated Kai and Lucia with restraint in that respect. There was nothing they were particularly good at, and as they lacked the imagination to think of anything very special, this deficiency, if it could be called that, did not bother them. The circus had been their world since birth, and it was natural that it should remain so. Kai had wanted to become a clown but lacked the fathomless melancholy and the terrible equilibrium between inward-directed altruism and outward-directed self-hate which is the hallmark of that profession, and therefore nothing had come of it. A clown must at all times be able to maim, corrupt and distort his own body, but the body in which Kai resided continued to shine through every mutilation, so that he was incapable of eliciting that tear-mingled laughter which a clown needs in order to exist.

Something similar was the case with Lucia. She had set her heart on being a trapeze artiste, but her body lacked the inner contradiction that allows the audience to endure the thought that the trapeze artiste may, at any moment, crash to her death. This possibility is always implied and is the first prerequisite of the spectator's enjoyment, which includes both the fear and the hope that the catastrophe will actually occur. With regard to Lucia, in some spectators the fear was too great and in others the hope was too slight. This hope derives from the fact that the spectator knows that the person leaping through the air high above is not really able to fly. The punishment is the fall, and the fact that no fall occurs is the miracle.

With Lucia it was different. Her parents had taught her the art and she was not afraid, but as soon as spectators were present, a strange, perhaps chemical reaction occurred. The fearful among them truly did not want that body, of which they immediately acknowledged the uniqueness and therefore the utter impossibility of having such a body themselves, to end up as a mangled mess of excrement and blood, especially not in front of their eyes. The hopeful ones had a different problem. They believed that someone with such a body must indeed be able to fly, and the fact that it never flew farther than the next trapeze or into the arms of those who had begotten it was a bitter disappointment. What should have been admiration turned into boredom; the vision of blood and death, which offers so much enjoyment, became irrelevant and the boredom quickly turned to distaste, which is a state of affairs no circus manager can tolerate for long. A life outside the big top was equally inconceivable, and therefore Kai and Lucia appeared, under their own names, as illusionists.

I think it would be improper to intervene yet again between reader and narrative. On the other hand, I myself am the narrator, and there are times when I can no longer

17

bear the loneliness of this classroom, where I sit squeezed in a school desk like a bloated eight-year-old. Of course I could use the teacher's desk, but then I would be facing the empty classroom, and to me the pupil's view is the natural one—otherwise I would have become a teacher myself. No one knows it, and yet it is true that a man alone, even someone of my age, plays games when he is sure no one is looking and when the volume of silence becomes too great to bear. August in Zaragoza is as bad as cycling in the desert. It isn't so much the heat that troubles me, but the silence in a space intended for noise, the ridiculously empty playground outside the window and these childless desks around me.

I have taken the desk that used to be mine of old, the second-to-last one on the right-hand side, and if you could see me there, you would understand why no book of mine has ever been reviewed in *El País*. Children don't write books; children play games, and so do I. Look and see. I pretend I am moving my blue, substantial shadow toward the door, which I open to allow an even more intangible shadow to enter, to whom—to which—I talk, though only very briefly.

I read very little fiction, although I know exactly what Delibes and Goytisolo and Cela and all those people are doing. Poetry I always have near me, even the younger poets such as Pere Gimferrer and Anibal Nuñez. I don't know much about Dutch literature; in the days when I studied in the Netherlands I didn't have much time. And here you can buy nearly anything, of course. I very much like Multatuli's *Ideas*, although they are not particularly Dutch, and also a strange book by someone who I am told is a geologist, a book about a conceivable God. Most of the other books I have read seem to be imitations of reality, stories from daily life, and you can hear those in any bar. I don't care much for that. When I pay my twice-monthly visits to the ministry in Madrid, I always try to buy a Dutch newspaper. Most of them are poor stuff, but there are two that can compare in quality with *El País*. Here again it strikes me that the Dutch, for all their consistency, always call things differently from what they are. One of these papers is decidedly not for the people, so it is called *Volkskrant,* the "people's paper." The other is clearly read by intellectuals and is called *Handelsblad,* "trade news"! I sometimes read book reviews or interviews with writers, and what strikes me is their metaphysical pretentiousness. Either they write secret diaries, which are then published, or texts that are clearly about themselves; but despite a certain pathos, these do not overflow the banks of daily life. They claim they want to "leave a trace" as though Proust had not already taught us that books, like their authors, die.

For the rest I like the Brahmin poetry of Adwaita, and the alchemist crypto script of Achterberg, though I sometimes have difficulty in following him. But my true love is philosophy, though I increasingly suspect philosophers of being failed poets. They have a great feeling for systems, but, alas, usually not for language. I like the webs they spin, though it seems to me they are forever writing variants on Plato, and so, when I am somewhere in a remote part of the province, and the whole country is dying the siesta death, I read, over and over again, those same old dialogues that never bore me.

What else do I read? Diaries, letters and, best of all, dictionaries. For let us be honest: without the intervention of any thinking agent, language itself is still the greatest communicator.

"Do you remember what you wanted to say?" asks my wife at such a moment, for I am inclined to digress and run on like a mill race. "You were going to open a door; you were letting someone in, weren't you?"

There we are again, language. In Spanish we say, *Hablar más que una urraca,* run on like a magpie. I look at Van Goor's Spanish-Dutch dictionary and see that *urraca* is *ekster,* magpie. Followed by: *to run on like a blind finch*! How does a magpie change into a finch between Spain and the Netherlands? But it isn't a finch; it's a blind finch. And that is not a bird; it is a type of food. Not that they would ever eat a finch in the Netherlands, because that isn't allowed. A blind finch is a rolled-up slice of meat with mincemeat inside. Who knows? Perhaps there are blind finches that run on. I haven't got as far as that yet.

I must let my shadow in. Two dictionaries I always have with me when I settle down here in August are the *Diccionario de la Lengua Española* and the *New Webster's Encyclopedic Dictionary of the English Language.* At the moment when the black hole of the board in front of me suggests that every illusion of meaning has receded from my story and that, if I stare for long enough into the void, there will appear on its gray slate surface a story that, if I could translate it, would be universally acclaimed as a masterpiece—at such moments of absentia and, for me, uncharacteristic despair, I open *Webster's.* That "letting in" was a somewhat cumbersome comparison; but to me, certainly when I am alone and allow myself a playful moment, Noah Webster is a person. Something shatters now. My faithful friend has nothing to say about illusionists, at least not about mine. Kai and Lucia are not mentioned! What it says is precisely the reverse:

one given to illusion. Wrong! That refers to the spectator only. The illusionist stands on the stage and gives; the spectator is deceived or participates in the deceit, and receives. *To illude: the act of deceiving and imposing upon; illusion: deception, mockery, a deceptive appearance, an unreal vision presented to the bodily or mental eye.* No trace of the culprit. He crops up again in Van Goor, and like the magpie and the finch, he too has lost a feather over the Pyrenees and now has only one *l.*

Ilusionista, goochelaar, conjuror, illusionist. There he gets his *l* back, but then he is no more than a conjuror; and although this is someone who beguiles the senses, we are used to his doing so by means of material objects such as cards and balls that fly through the air and obey an extreme, curved form of gravity, handkerchiefs that have their vanishing point close by, that kind of thing. Spanish and Dutch often reinforce each other, but not this time, though I have made one small gain: that strange, exotic sound of the word *goo-chel,* conjure, and the secret pride that with my throat inherited from the Moors, I can pronounce that *ch* as harshly as any native of the Dutch North.

People who in the old days used to visit real theatres and circuses still remember this kind of act. Lucia would stand blindfolded on the stage or in the arena, while Kai stood among the audience, firing questions at her about the man or woman he was looking at and whose name, age and appearance she would unfailingly divine. The fact that these details always matched the information stated on the passport or identity card Kai had been given by the person concerned was the miracle that in an earlier age or, as we shall see, in less enlightened regions enraptured the public.

21

How did they do it? I myself come from a province where, owing to the vastness of the landscape and the remoteness of the villages, the supernatural has not altogether disappeared, and at a sight of this nature I would prefer simply to believe in the inexplicable and leave it at that. One should allow obscurity to exist, certainly in its minor forms, for it is part of us, like night is a part of time, although some people will object to this mixing of categories.

But no, it was a talent, and although the shadow of the inexplicable had been woven into it, I know enough about the mysterious and yet natural web of rising and falling pitch, pauses, choice of words, hesitations, interjections and musical accents with which they constantly captivated and amazed their public, to be able to say with confidence that Kai and Lucia played a complicated game with their audience, a game subject to iron laws, like nature itself. To the spectators such considerations did not count. They felt they were dealing with one person rather than two, however far removed the two manifestations might be from each other at any one time. Two in one, two halves seeking, finding, if not becoming each other—ever since Plato's *Symposium* a dream-wish that was here somehow made visible, or at least hinted at. And this led to rapture, for that was what one saw in their faces. The apparent extraordinariness of these happenings, which like writing and politics (but not road building) are to some extent based on trickery, matched the extraordinariness of their appearance, so that all in all they were a great asset to the circus.

The circus itself was not doing too well. First, there was the recession, a word that managed to conceal the fact that people were better off now than any generation had ever been before. Second, we were then living in a time when anything that could be expressed by the body without intervention of electronics and in the embarrassing presence of other bodies appeared to lose its validity. Gestures had to be seen in as many living rooms as possible at exactly the same moment by people who were not physically present; and the natural sound of the human voice prompted an irritable reaction, as if for the first time since creation this sound, or the ear receiving it, suddenly lacked something essential, a lack that had never been noticed by anyone in all the preceding centuries.

People no longer played games at home or, to put it more clearly, played together; nor did they go out to watch other people playing. More and more circuses closed down, and the clowns, illusionists and bear tamers vanished into the great void into which basket weavers, pavement artists, street actors, knife grinders, storytellers, falconers and fairground folk had preceded them. Longinus, referring to a few weak passages in Herodotus and Theopompus (an inflated name I would love to be mine), once warned that the sublime can easily be marred by the trivial. But how is this stylistic problem to be solved in a story that has as its subject the marring of the sublime by the trivial? We shall see. In the end, says Horace, you can always destroy what you have not yet published, but once the words have been dispatched, you cannot bring them back. That was true then and it is still true now. It is the notion of perfection that keeps troubling me as I write this story, because I do not think anyone believes in it any longer, certainly not my publisher in León. With the death of God, whether he ever existed or not, our model of perfection has vanished. Since then, art has elongated the body created in his image and likeness, divided it into sections, drilled holes in it and distorted it. It looks as though we can no longer tolerate perfection, not even as an idea, because it bores us like a dream too often dreamed. It is emptier than usual in this classroom today.

After the circus in which Kai and Lucia worked had been dismantled for the last time, at which some newspapers had shed a few crocodile tears, they appeared for some time in small theatres and community halls. But one day they received a letter from their manager in Rotterdam inviting them—summoning would be a better word—in order, as he put it, to discuss "an important plan."

There are popes that look like professional crooks and whores that seem as if they never knew the world, but Kai and Lucia's impresario, who was called Reier, really looked like an impresario. He smoked fat black cigars, hand rolled by simple people in distant lands, so that he was always slightly withdrawn from sight. This was just as well, for he had a grubby skin that hung slackly about his large face, in which the eyes, unlike those of real predators, deliberately avoided their prey. The prey was always whoever was sitting in front of him.

In an interview, he had once let it be known that everyone was replaceable, including his wife, and he meant it. It was a rule from which he had exempted only himself. Kai and Lucia's act brought him very little revenue, and the hope of ever forcing his massive body onto Lucia's he had long since given up, even if only out of laziness; but as long as he thought there was a chance of making a few coins out of them, he didn't let them go.

Fools, he thought, as he beckoned them to the chairs in front of his desk. As always when they were not on their own together, or with friends or among a crowd, Kai and Lucia felt unsure.

"Children," said Reier across his cloud of doom, "let's be frank with each other. What you two do is highly professional, it's polished, it has class, no one else can do it. You are still young and you are beautiful (too beautiful, he thought). I have always worked with your parents; you know your craft down to your fingertips, but the job is no longer what it was. What you do is special, but small. And most people don't care about it any more. They can get the pick of the whole world on their television screens every day, and they won't shift their backsides to leave the house. At home they can smoke and drink or do whatever they want, and they get the best shows from Las Vegas into the bargain. They come out of their holes only for sex or if they have to pay through the nose, because that's status. Sex shows we've discussed before. You don't want that." He slavered at the thought of Lucia with three old fellows in monks' habits or Kai in a mud bath with a fat Negress; but they'd never agree, and having them perform together as a couple was even more impossible, because that would then eliminate the essential ingredient of such shows: humiliation.

"What I have to say to you is very sad. Ve-ry sad." He said it once more for good measure. Give them a good fright first, then strike. "I see no solution, unless . . ."

He got up, went to the window and looked out over Rotterdam. What a city, he thought admiringly.

Lucia moved closer to Kai and he put his arm around her shoulders. "Unless what?" asked Kai in the tone of someone who flinches at nothing.

Of course the mug would bite, thought Reier. "Unless you two are prepared to work in the South," replied the blue nylon-suited back by the window. "I don't believe in mincing my words."

This was no superfluous addition, for in the trade "going to work in the South" meant you were finished for good. "So and so has gone to work in the South"—the only thing you would ever hear of him after that was the news of his death, if you heard anything at all.

"Otherwise I am afraid I can do nothing further for you."

Faster than you would expect of such a large body, he turned around, already stood near them, embraced them in his bear hug and whispered, "I'm so sorry about it, my dears. I am so terribly sorry about it. We have always worked so well together, but there's nothing I can do. It's either this or nothing. The times are against us. It's the times."

It was as if he reeled under the blow he was dealing, but he kept himself standing by holding on extra firmly to Lucia.

What a girl, he thought, and said, "Do you know who has gone to the South these last months?" and before they could answer, he rattled off a long list of clowns, conjurors, ventriloquists and jugglers whose faded portraits still hung in the corridor outside his office. They had left the protective North of their former successes and were now performing somewhere far away in those strange regions, in theatres with dirty dressing rooms of which no northern newspaper would ever mention the names.

Lucia bowed her head, a shower of gold. Reier felt a tear on his hand, and the tiny coolness of this sorrow consisting of only one drop of water so burned into his skin that even he understood he should let go of her. The window, he thought, was perhaps the best place after all.

Kai looked at a circus poster from the nineteenth century, in which Schmidt's Menagerie, the Greatest in All Europe, announced the appearance of the "Terrible Asiatic Lion in Association with the Blood-thirsty Hyena and the Gigantic Elephant Miss Fanny, 130 years old."

"Would we be appearing in circuses?" he asked.

Reier turned around, but not too fast this time, for he knew he had a bite.

"In tents and theatres," he said. He put his cigar, now suddenly a big wet object, on the desk and said, "It's yes or no. Here I can't do much for you. I could sell you just once on TV and that might keep you ticking for a while, but after that it's finished, done with. You must decide for yourselves. Some of my people are at this moment preparing for a kind of tour starting in Dachfart, and they'll be setting off soon. Dachfart is in the mountains just below the passes. To the South." He pointed at the map behind his desk, on which the stubborn, outsize balloon of the seemingly vast-looking South hung like an overripe, pompous fruit from the narrow, fragile corridor that began in Limburg and ran down as far as the mountains and that, whatever northerners might claim in their purblindness, formed an inalienable part of the kingdom.

History, too, can be sick at times, and the course of such sicknesses can best be observed in historical atlases, in which countries proliferate, burst, protrude, scatter, wither and shrink in all colors and shades across and within their former frontiers. No, the Kingdom of the Netherlands was not a pretty sight. It looked as if someone had throttled the narrow neck of the strip along the Maas and the Rhine and shaken it furiously, resulting in a massive internal hemorrhage that had made the bit below the fist swell monstrously so that now it dangled like a

27

silly loose sack, containing dark, desolate and no doubt dangerous territories in which provincial borders seemed to have been drawn at random. The sack began somewhere northeast of Locarno and had, so it seemed, been flung against defenseless Albania with such force that the underbelly of the kingdom resembled the scalloped edges of a pig's intestines. If you looked at it long enough, you involuntarily started praying your *ende-vers*, as they say in the South. But Kai and Lucia hadn't got as far as that yet.

"I can't see the point," said Kai.

"All right, so you can't see the point." Reier sat down on the edge of his chair and relit his cigar. He liked the mixture of dead ashes and his own spittle gone cold. The smoke was now blacker and announced more doom. "Let me put it a different way then: you see no point in going there, and there is no point in staying here. There everything is new. It's a new country to you. No one knows you there."

"No one lives there either."

"An artiste should never say that. There are people there. People are audience. Perhaps they are different from us, but they are Dutch and they speak the same language, or at any rate they understand you. You have free access there. You're allowed to work there. And anyway, if the queen can go there, so can you."

It was true. The sight of their monarch in one of her exuberant hats—as if the never-worn crown of precious metal had changed into textile or finely plaited cane, thereby acquiring the right to expand in all directions—amid dancing and cheering southerners had made the northerners feel slightly embarrassed at the carefree joy in which they themselves would have liked to participate but which seemed to be forever denied to them. And although these royal excursions did not take place very often, the head of state seemed to enjoy them immensely, as though the people she encountered there embodied the pure essence of the notion of "subject," the natural corollary of her own extraordinary form of existence. That the somewhat sombre, withdrawn man at her side was unable to share in her ecstasy did not seem to bother her. Thanks to her peculiar, inherited function she had been called to a kind of mystical union with her people, and whatever else you might say about them, her people they were.

"I'm sending you to Dachfart," said Reier, "Anhovet, Doremenen, Touchtlake, Barech, Slaec." The names, always exotic to a northerner, flowed from his lips. "Small towns, but towns with theatres nevertheless. And a theatre," he added tautologically, "is a theatre, wherever it may be. Or would you rather work in an office?"

Lucia clenched her fists. Had these been cast, not by nature in their temporary form but by Ghiberti in bronze, they would have fetched millions at Sotheby's. She sighed. In the topsy-turvy reality artistes live in, a world in which you are not allowed to dress up and where you therefore have to be yourself all the time, whatever that may be, is the first vision of hell.

"I don't like the idea," said Kai. "Perhaps we ought to talk to someone else, if you have nothing for us. I have a friend in the Army Recreational Section . . . "

"And they would send you to the South just the same— if they want you at all, since they use only films these days. And anyway, how would you like that, with her, entertaining a bunch of famished wolves that are bored out of their stupid minds? There are more troops down there than here."

This was also true. The southern independence move-

29

ment had already cost the lives of a number of military police and civil servants. It had not yet become a truly popular movement, but the police could no longer cope unaided, certainly not since a lenient government had given the South its own police corps, which, especially in the lower ranks, consisted mainly of southerners. The next government, alarmed by the increasing violence, had sent in the army, which carried out its task more or less grudgingly. Every military casualty was given maximum publicity in the North, so that before long, opinion polls showed that the vast majority of northerners would much rather get rid of the southern provinces than keep them.

"When we come back," said Kai, "if we ever do come back, everyone will have forgotten us."

"Is it beautiful there?" asked Lucia.

The idea of beauty in connection with the southern Netherlands was unusual. Just as the southerners thought the North was flat, gray and windy, so the Dour Ones, as the people north of the passes were nicknamed, regarded the South as desolate, wild and malevolent. And the inhabitants backward—that went without saying. If you had no business there, you didn't go.

"Beautiful," said Reier, thinking of rancid food, dusty roads, snowy passes and an icy wind that cut off your breath in the winter, "what is beautiful? That is different for everyone. You are a little dreamer, and you have chosen a hard trade in a hard world. But it's your livelihood. Beautiful . . . there are mountains, and I don't like mountains. But theatres are beautiful, and there are still theatres there. And for people who still have a spirit of adventure in their blood, it's a great experience."

Kai stood up. "We'll think about it," he said.

When they had left the room, Reier dialed a long number. Someone answered. "It's okay," said Reier, "they're coming."

He articulated the words very slowly, as if he were speaking to someone who was deaf, or to a very small child.

6

CAMINO, *carretera,* way, street, road. It has always intrigued me that in Dutch the word *weg,* way, also means away, absent. In Spanish *el camino* is not only the road but also the journey. Now a journey is by definition also the absence from the place you have set out from, but the brutal directness of *away* is not contained in it. In my profession I have, of course, philosophized often enough about roads in all their meanings, for whether it is *via, carretera, camino*, path or street, these words are always, in any decent explanatory dictionary, followed by a procession of idiomatic and allegorical expressions that make you think, especially when your life consists, as mine does, of roads and is largely spent on roads. The notion that virtually all roads between Delft, Zaragoza, Isfahan and Peking are connected with one another opens up such dizzying labyrinthine perspectives that I can scarcely stay quietly in my seat. But it is not question of *my* life. I leave this page, though it is with a sigh. I just don't think that roads are thought about often enough.

Today is an important day for Kai and Lucia. The

clock of their destiny has been wound and will, until the end of their story, go on ticking with its measured, calculated beat, which, according to some, will continue even when we are no longer here to perceive that time exists.

They left, and after several days' traveling are now approaching the mountains that lift the road up, sucking it toward them. You feel this when you are in a small car; your destination is no longer before you but above you and, in hairpin bends, sometimes behind you. This is bound to create a sense of confusion and, as with Kai and Lucia, fear. There was enough to be afraid of. To those born on the plain, where everything can be surveyed, mountains stand between them and the view. That which blocks the view becomes itself the view, and this is oppressive. Besides, it was autumn, gloomy and cold. Strands of mist drifted menacingly past sheer rock faces; the tree line, that last link with the familiar, was now below them, and they were driving amid stone: heaps, towers, walls and swords of stone. They tried to cheer each other up with lighthearted chatter or with small gestures and touches, but as the emptiness of the landscape became greater, so it became quieter in the car. There were virtually no more villages; the few houses they still saw from time to time were of a different style; the sparse vegetation seemed to have adopted the character of the landscape, hard, malevolent. That evening they were to reach the pass where the Union frontier divided the fatherland into its uneven parts.

"It gets dark later here," said Kai, but Lucia did not reply. The sun was a harsh, whitish blur among the dirty clouds, and after another interminable bend the mountain range ahead of them looked like a vicious row of lower teeth, monstrous fangs pointed like prehistoric marble axheads. It was unimaginable that the road would lead through these. When the last light vanished behind the jaw with a dramatic display of purple and blood red rags, they both thought (but did not say) that, invisible in the darkness, another row of teeth was sure to hang, similar but downward pointing, ready to slam shut and crush everything that moved within the dragon's mouth. They crept closer to each other. There were few oncoming cars, but after each one that passed, having announced itself long in advance by a distant roving gleam that flared up in all directions, it was as if the world had become even darker and more mysterious.

It was a long time before they saw a few fixed lights, yellow and dim. This is the last moment at which we can still turn back, thought Lucia, but again she did not speak. The village they entered was deserted. Everyone was dead, gone or in bed. They stopped at what seemed to be the only inn. In a corner of the bar a few men were playing cards. Their eyes followed Lucia, making her feel as though they were gnawing at her. The only familiar things were the advertisements for Heineken and Bols. Everything else—the voices, the furniture, even the color of the light—seemed strange, as though the territory they were about to enter the next day was already refusing them, or warning them—that was also possible.

Their room was small and cold. The bed looked slept in, and on the wall hung a ludicrous print of a girl on a reindeer. Lucia stood forlornly by the window and looked out. There was no longer anything to see, and yet she felt the presence of the invisible mountains.

"I am afraid," she said, but it was worse than that. No longer a feeling that came over her, it was a state that had taken possession of her whole body, a substance, so that every part of her—eyes, skin, feet—had become fear, a fear that could be driven out only if she now turned back, ran down the stairs, through the bar where those men would try to block her way, and then outside, into the car, away, back to the low flat world she ought never to have left.

"You're tired," said Kai. "Tomorrow everything will be different." But when they woke after a restless night during which a fierce wind had suddenly risen, tugging at the window like a man trying to get in and, thought Lucia, a randy laugh had rung out outside their door, everything was still the same.

Kai was the first to get up. He had dreamed that a splinter of glass or an infinitesimal, sharp piece of ice had got into his eye, and when he woke he thought this was the reason why a veil lay over all he could see. He opened the torn, thin curtains and saw it was not true. Daylight itself was the veil. A color of gray slime hung over the landscape. Liquid mud, a syrupy substance spreading slowly over houses and cars, a substance, he thought, that, once it had touched you, would stick to you forever.

7

FEAR and reluctance are feelings one should not give in to, thought Kai, mistakenly. The falsifications that result from such resistance often cause more trouble than if one had simply bowed to one's fear, but he was too young or merely not clever enough to know this. I didn't mean to write this, yet now I have. Sometimes I mutter to myself, why must it always slip out? I have invented him myself, after all, for who else decides that he is now walking out of the room on tiptoe so as not to wake Lucia? He gently closes the door behind him and goes downstairs.

The innkeeper was more talkative than on the evening before and asked about the purpose of their journey. Kai told him they were going across the border to perform, a word he had to explain further. When he had done so, the innkeeper advised him earnestly to go back.

"It's no good you going over there, my boy, certainly not together with her. I am not from the North myself, but I can tell you, it's a right bear garden over on the other side. They're savages, nothing less; your life isn't safe. Some of the people that stop off here, well, I have to let them in, it's my living, but then I sleep with a knife under my pillow at night. You northerners take it for granted that if anything happens you can phone the police. Well, we have the border police here. Take a good look at them; then you'll think differently."

How strange, thought Kai, that the thing which should have inspired the greatest confidence in those policemen was precisely what made them so frightening. Their uniforms were either too big or too small, and all were dirty and slovenly, but this was not the worst. Their heads, which he saw in profile or full face, looked like those of criminals in police records, and this curious contradiction between physiognomy and uniform heightened the terror-inspiring effect, which was reinforced still further by the large old-fashioned revolvers that hung loosely in their holsters.

"What kind of people are they?"

"They are the border guards. They belong on the other side. I'd rather not have them in here, but they eat one meal a day here."

"Border guards? But if it's one country, why should there be a border?"

"You may well ask! It's the only way of keeping track of what goes from South to North. We don't get many show-biz people here actually. Well, maybe they drive through, or they go by air; but most of the people that pass by here do stop, even if only for a moment, because it's the last stop, and on the other side it's not much fun."

He beckoned Kai closer to his unshaven face. "If ever you should be in trouble, those are the last people you should turn to. At the very least it would cost you money, and they usually cause all the trouble themselves in the first place."

Kai decided to say nothing of all this to Lucia. When

he returned to their room, he saw she had hidden under the blankets. Gently he pulled the dingy rags away from her and was, as always, moved by her beauty. The golden hair lay like a dazzling glow on the grubby pillow. He wanted to stroke her, but she had withdrawn into her sorrow; her body reacted as if it were someone else's and her eyes were blurred as if she had been crying ever since he had left the room. He pretended not to notice, hummed, walked to the window with the springy tread of someone going to meet a tremendous adventure, and looked out over the chilly open road that led to the border post.

8

SOMEONE who has never, by whim or necessity, made a journey to the southernmost limit of the Netherlands cannot imagine the shock most northerners experience the first time they travel across the Twosplant Pass, the first of the High Passes. Even those who always complain about the boring dullness of the marsh delta feel here as though their world is being broken in two.

So there they stood. In the customhouse there was admittedly a portrait of the queen on the wall, full-length. Festooned with medals and without her customary smile, she had more of an air of surprise, as if she wondered why she had to stand here alone in this shack with only the fair-haired man in tails by her side, looking as if he had just come in to tell her they had run out of wine. Perhaps the reason why she was not smiling was that she wanted to make it clear it was not her fault that some of her more eccentric ancestors had taken it into their heads to rule over the barren desert on the other side of the border.

The building itself was a dilapidated, shabby hut. One

of the men Kai had seen in the inn that morning came outside.

"Out you get," he said to Lucia.

"Why?" asked Kai. "Here are our papers. Besides, we're not leaving the country."

The man took no notice of him and banged against the car.

"Hurry up."

Lucia got out and followed the man into the hut. They disappeared into a room. There he took hold of her and ran his big hands over her breasts and between her legs and then sat down on a chair and leaned back.

"What was that for?" asked Lucia.

"A little frisk," he said cheerfully.

"I want to make a complaint."

"Complaints in triplicate to the commander of the guard. Maybe he'll say I haven't been thorough enough. We have other ways, too, you know. We have a lady for that." He got up slowly.

At that moment Kai burst into the room, dragging one of the other policemen along by the arm.

"Dearie me," said the first one, "what a hurry we are in. Never mind, we wanted you in here anyway. Passport, car documents."

"What's going on here?"

"Papers!"

"You'd better hand them over," said Lucia softly.

"Very sensible, you have a sensible wife. Right, that's two hundred guilders."

"What for?"

The policemen looked at each other in amazement.

"Don't they always ask silly questions!" said the man who had searched Lucia.

40

"Two hundred guilders. Otherwise you stay a little longer."

Kai took two hundred guilders out of his wallet.

"You'll get them back when you come through here again. If you ever do."

"I want a receipt."

"The day after tomorrow."

Lucia held out her hand to Kai. He picked up his passport, which no one had looked at, from the desk and put it back into his pocket. Slowly they went outside.

"Very sensible people," they heard, before the door fell shut behind them. They returned to the car in silence. The barrier went up and without looking at the grinning faces behind the window they drove into the southern Netherlands.

9

AGAINST the backdrop of a landscape and a mood, three things now happen in quick succession. The landscape on the other side of the pass is merciless. "In such places many similar instances of charm could be demonstrated," says Demetrius in his essay on style, and this applies equally, of course, to the converse of charm, ugliness. It is tempting at this point to expatiate once more on the overpowering effect of mountains, especially when you enjoy doing so, but I will say no more than that they are merciless and that this influences Kai and Lucia's mood.

As they gyrate through unrelenting bends, Kai begins to feel sick, so they have to stop. This they do by the side of a ravine and as he stands outside the car, the icy wind blows a speck of dust, grit, glass, into his eye, just as his dream had predicted. He tries to see what it is in the driving mirror. When you have something in your eye, you cannot see yourself clearly, you look through a watery blur and see in the mirror someone with a different eye from the one you are used to, or perhaps you see your eye for the first time. I think that when people look at their faces they do not look at their eyes, they avoid them even though they do see them. If, like Kai at this moment, they are forced to look at their eyes from close by, they see a strange, separate thing which is an eye, with its reddish flush of blood, and this is a frightening sight. But worse still: if that with which you see becomes different, perhaps everything becomes different, including yourself. Something of this sort is happening to Kai. Is he now suddenly a different person? No, of course not. A notch has been carved in the whole that he was, a *wunde,* as someone in a castle in the South will later call it, and as with every wound, however small, part of what one is disappears into it. Soon afterward, therefore, he takes a bend too widely and hits the rock face, so that the left fender is crushed against the front wheel and they are unable to drive on. Now they are standing still in the silent landscape. For a long time no one passes. Then they both hear the sound of an engine, but they cannot judge from which direction it comes. They get out into the road to flag down the car. The sound disappears behind the rocks, re-emerges, disappears again and returns more strongly.

What appears at last is a large black Tatra, a Czech car resembling an animal more than anything else, the only car with a dorsal fin, a beast of prey. It does not stop, but in the second of its passing they see the white, icy cold, sharply outlined profile of a woman. As if cut out of ice, thinks Lucia, and the image is correct. Not only that; it is, together with the passing of the car, part of the natural order. Everything happens like that here. They will miss their first performance in Dachfart, and that, too, belongs in the natural order.

Another car approaches, with three border guards in

it. These are different: they are inquisitive; they want to see suitcases, papers, everything. One holds Lucia's sequined dress in front of his uniform and takes a dancing step, and this, against the background of bare mountains, is funny.

The second one says nothing, lets the fabric slide through his fingers, and looks at Lucia. The third is friendly. He wants to know what they do, and asks for a demonstration. This becomes their first performance in the South. The wind tugs at their clothes; the cold bites. The guard has handed Kai a gray-colored document. Kai has blindfolded Lucia; she is standing some distance away and is afraid of falling into the ravine. An expression of deep concentration now appears on Kai's face. He peers at the paper, circles his left hand over it as if to cast a spell on it, then makes the same circular movements with his right hand. The eyes of the three men follow his every move. Then he raises his head, a little heroically. From the cosmos there comes a message that, by force of mind, he must pass on to Lucia, for she alone can decipher it.

"Are you ready?"

"Yes."

"Can you feel the force?"

"Yes." She raises a slightly trembling hand.

"What am I holding, Lucia, what am I holding?"

"Gray . . ."

"Yes."

"Paper . . . a little book?"

"Yes?"

After the change in pitch and the question mark she hesitates. While this scene is taking place and I am describing it (such things happen simultaneously), I wonder

44

whether semeiologists have ever occupied themselves with the code language of illusionism. Lucia's golden hair flutters around the blindfold. She sees that the men do not know at whom to look.

"What does it say on it?"

"A number."

"How many figures does the number have?" So that must be seven.

"Er . . . seven figures."

"And what is the number?"

"Two . . . three . . . "

"Two, three . . . and then?"

"Nine."

"Good."

"Six."

"Four more figures."

"Five."

"Very good."

"Seven, six."

Applause, supported by a gust of wind. Kai removes her blindfold, and she shakes her hair. She looks radiant. A theatre full of people or three men on a country road, it makes no difference. She has performed, she has altered her surroundings by a fraction, she has shifted something in the day. Minimally, but still. Now she is as happy as a writer who has told a fairy tale and has not interrupted himself in doing so. All these things they take away from us; all we are left with are the frayed tatters of former visions. Shut up, Tiburón!

The three men prize the fender away from the wheel with a steel bar—that is their magic art. An hour or two later, preceded by the police car, Kai and Lucia enter Dachfart. Dark colonnades, signposts indicating Amsterdam followed by a four-figure number, and, for the rest, impossible names, old American cars, a road surface riddled with holes. But also, thought Kai—though only because I want him to—an air of cheerfulness, clusters of men in poorly lit cafés, carts of fruit and steaming meat above a flickering fire. When they arrive at the dilapidated theatre, it is Lucia, not he, who notices one of the border guards drawing the other's attention, with a nod of the head, to the black Tatra, and the other shrugging his shoulders. She remembers the face of the woman, and shivers, as if the woman and the evening air were the same.

10

THE director of the theatre is sweating, the whole theatre smells of sweat and makeup. This is as it should be, the counterweight to fans and eau de cologne. To Kai and Lucia there are no longer any mountains, no cold and no South. There are only nervous people scurrying around the corridors backstage, made-up or half-made-up faces, quick exchanges of jokes and banter, the deep glow of fake jewelry, the mask and huge shoes of a clown, the tuning of instruments. Nothing is real and therefore everything is right. They are given a small dressing room: the water from the tap has the color of diluted blood, there are bits of cotton balls lying about streaked with the black mud of other people's mascara, the mirror is cracked and fractures their perfect reflection. What they feel is agitation—all the rest is unimportant. What they hear, just as a sailor hears the sea in the distance, is the sound, inaudible to others, of the audience, a live animal that will either eat them or spew them out. The dress, which held up against the border guard's uniform had been an obscene flag, glitters in the dingy light. Kai's costume is a misconceived version of something baroque; it gleams; it is black with a purple sheen, designed to match the color of his hair. He powders his face white and becomes uglier in order that he may be more beautiful on the stage, a perverse form of beauty based on its own denial, like actors from the twenties who moved their mouths but brought forth no sound.

A bang on the door and it is their turn. They position themselves in the wings and watch how the clown, a fat old man, tries to catch a ball he himself has thrown up in the air. But the ball, which represents fate, is itself a person. It is the clown's opponent. It teases, evades, escapes, pushes the clown, who becomes ever older, ever more dejected, and finally, in a last effort to control the recalcitrant world, falls, amid loud cheers, headlong on the floor and crawls away wailingly on all fours, past the legs of Kai and Lucia, who now make their entrance. Silence descends, and it is a silence they know, the silence of an audience that is becoming conscious of its own paltriness. They are too beautiful, and they have only a few minutes in which to make amends for this, minutes that will decide between love and hatred. And moreover, they are a pair. I have always loved the Dutch word *paar*, pair. The Spanish word is too long. *Pareja*—when you say it loudly enough, it does indeed bind, but it never becomes such an absolute bond as *paar*. The pair is the smallest human union that exists, and therefore, because it excludes others, it is insufferable. It is a platonic idea, and this cannot be endured in reality, certainly not when, in the case of Kai and Lucia, it looks as though the idea is invulnerable, *blamelees* once again. It ought to have remained a possibility; it must not stand on a stage, unless it triumphs.

While, from behind, the director's voice introduces them, Kai walks into the auditorium. He does not hear the voice, which now says "And watch out! If you have anything dangerous with you, anything of a compromising nature, anything that no one else may see or know about, put it away, far away, for every piece of paper, every document, every letter touched by Kai, can be seen, spelled and read out by Lucia. Through the magic power that he transfers to her, she sees everything, without eyes, everything, without exception!"

It is, Kai has already noticed, a good audience. They believe; they are not yet spoiled. Like a peacock he stands among the ranks, selects his victims, decides whom he should and should not choose. His appearance, his close proximity, his northern accent—these things excite. All eyes move from him to the emblematic woman on the stage, a blonde woman who sways gently in the light as if even now she is already being moved by mysterious forces and who, behind her veil of darkness, seems to suck in the names and figures that are passed on to her. Is it a trick, or is he sending digit after digit, letter after letter, through the invisible air? And, worse thought, do they see more than they say, those two sorcerers; do they also know the other, darker secrets that everyone carries within him?

At the back of the hall, in a box, sits the woman from the Tatra. Kai sees her only when he is already too close, when it is too late. She is not alone in the box.

"Don't be embarrassed, man, just get on with your story!" This I say to myself, here in Zaragoza, or rather to a part of myself, to the engineer, to the person who always wants to justify himself. I would not last long as an illusionist! How can it be that I can see what happens

49

in that box? Stupid question, and too late. How can it be that I went on that journey, that I saw what Kai did not see, that the border guard molested Lucia? How do I know what they think? It is as though Kai were telling his audience how he does his illusionist's act, and that is the worst kind of audience abuse there is; it is against all the rules. It undermines faith; it spoils enjoyment. I won't do it again. It is disruptive, a disturbance of the peace, a bad road surface.

But here we are already in the box. She is not alone, yet it is best to look first at her. There is no question of being able to guess her age. Ice, thought Lucia, but then with the appearance of the sort of ice that looks like glass, which the French have preserved in their word for ice, *glace*. This woman does not permit people to look at her in order to discover anything about her; her skin refracts one's gaze, and the thought that keeps hovering about her says that it is better so, for if the thought were to be admitted, then the onlooker would be pulled down to the icy cold underworld that exists beneath the glass.

She is the Snow Queen—that is what they call her. Without ever being able to put it into words, Kai will see it later: this woman belongs to the same category as Lucia, that of the perfect bodies, but her body is connected with death. She sees Kai approaching, like a spider expecting the fly. She says something to the older man beside her, who shakes his head, tries to dissuade, yet gives her a piece of paper for which she has asked him, shrugs his shoulders, does not want to know what she writes, does not want to see her give it to the younger man behind her in the box. The audience has to turn around in order to follow Kai as, in the beam of light that surrounds him, he walks toward her box.

When he, the woman and the two men are all caught in the circle of light, a sigh goes through the audience, as at a boxing match when after many lesser fights the moment arrives at last when the champions enter the ring. They know her. They had temporarily forgotten her, or maybe she was part of the evening's excitement simply by being present; but now they can no longer forget her. She sits like a frozen white doll; her jewels refract the spotlight and dazzle the young man standing before her, who knows he cannot turn back. They fixate upon each other, but not as equals. I can hear a pin drop.

11

LUCIA feels the pain in his eye, feels she has lost the audience. They breathe in the opposite direction. Through her untransparent blindfold she sees Kai's silhouette at the back of the hall. His body blots out the woman in the box, but Lucia knows she is there. She sees that the older man beside her, who has the face of an actor playing the role of an officer, would prefer not to be noticed. The second man she is unable to see. It is he who gives the piece of paper to Kai.

"Lucia, can you hear me?" the audience turns like a bull in the ring.

"Lucia?"

"Yes."

"I have here . . ." He turns around. Lucia averts her face, as if in a trance, and says, "A white piece of paper." The bull mutters, talks to itself, shakes its huge head.

"Can you see what is written on it?"

I am written on it; you are written on it. She thinks it but is not allowed to say it. He has taken a step sideways. She sees the woman, the young man behind her, eagerly bending forward. He is fair-haired but has something of the gypsy about him. He is enjoying himself.

"It comes from a man . . ."

"Yes . . . No . . ."

If we do not believe in the supernatural, and this we have agreed on, what then do we believe in? He has his code to let her know that it isn't working, that she will have to fend for herself as best she can. He can let her say what is written on the paper, but she is not allowed to say it.

Do I know what it says? Yes, I know what it says. Lucia can guess it. We don't say it. Dumas, père et fils, laugh at me. But no one in the audience knows what it says. No one, except the woman who wrote it and Kai who reads it. The power, if you want to call it that (I don't), which I have is that of a man all alone in a class-room, who is inventing something. Inventing is making decisions. Beyond that I can do nothing. Lucia stands motionless, facing the group in the box.

"No number . . . ?"

"No."

"Words, I see words."

"Yes."

She begins to tremble. He turns slowly and she does the only thing possible.

"They are . . . too strong . . ."

Then she falls, the way only an acrobat can fall, as in a slow-motion film. With infinite syrupiness her limbs fold; she coils in upon herself. On the same wooden floor where the humiliated clown crawled a few minutes earlier, an upright-standing woman collapses into a quivering pyramid of cloth that caves in ever further until it is an immobile human body lying on the stage, its head with the long hair artfully twisted forward so that the footlights give it a deep golden glow.

In a few steps Kai is with her, lifts her up, a peacock holding a peahen in his arms. He sets her down gently. She stands as if seeking an equilibrium in the air around her. The bull mutters. Then Kai quickly turns to the first row, so that the light briefly flashes in all the spangles of his costume; he snatches a document out of someone's ready hand, walks halfway down the central aisle and makes her say it: name, figures, age, height, eye color. Everyone can see it, it is correct, it is correct, and in a wave of cheering and applause they leave the stage, they come back once more, smiling, bowing, almost dancing to the tune of the pitiful orchestra.

The audience goes on clapping. Lucia has removed her blindfold. Kai looks at her questioningly and she nods. It is their custom, when the applause is strong enough, to take one more curtain call, separately, she last. She hears the applause and crosses Kai's path in the half-dark behind the stage. Then she stands alone in the light, as if she were drawing life from the hard, yokelish clapping, and leaves before it subsides. She does not see Kai backstage and goes to the dressing room.

The door is open, but he is not there. It is too soon to know for sure, and yet she knows. He is gone. She returns to the stage, where someone is now busy singing, and looks into the auditorium from the wings. The box is empty; the woman and her companions have gone. She wants to shout out his name but cannot, and looks for the exit leading to the public areas. When she has found it, she wanders in her suddenly foolish-looking dress through the semicircular corridors until she reaches the box. The door is open. She looks at the worn upholstery, sees the audience from behind, a world in reverse that increases her fear. She does not see the note lying under one of the seats. She runs backstage again, looks for the manager, cannot find him, goes past the door of her dressing room and enters the next one, that of the clown. The ball lies in the middle of the small room, much too big and yellow; the tall, curled-up shoes lean against an old suitcase; but the man in a long flannel vest sitting by the mirror cleaning off his makeup is an old woman.

12

KAI did not resist when the two men threw the heavy
black cloth over him; it happened too quickly. They
were not the same men as the ones in the box, he noticed,
but for the rest he remembered only the sharp, stupefying
smell of the cloth and the sensation of a long fall that
would never end, not even when he would know again
what was going on. And so that was what happened.

Even in the car he was still falling, and there was no
limit to the length of time it would continue. Now he was
lying in a room, motionless, forever falling, and although
there was still no limit to the time it would go on, within
the falling there were now differences. While his fall was
slow, other, quicker images flitted through him, and some
of these images were subject to a different gravitational
force from the one he had to obey; the point toward which
they were drawn was beside him, even above him, so that,
falling upwards, they crossed his path, thereby increasing
his dizziness and therefore his fear. Even when he kept
his eyes closed, he saw them, while his hand clutched at
the edge of the bed—the road, the hairpin bends, the

glow of the headlights of the Tatra, which had proved so much larger than it had appeared from the outside. Not only was he in it, squeezed between the two men, but she, too, was falling through his vision—the way she had been sitting in the car when he arrived, her face bearing the same expression as it had in the theatre. And she too was sitting between two men, but she was free.

How long had the journey lasted? He remembered darkness, light, and the same again, but there was no sequence. Now he sees himself by the roadside, humiliated, vomiting, and later, in the dark, squatting, while someone kicks him lightly in the loins with a shoe. Laughter also, but he only saw it; he did not hear it. It was not she who laughed. And she did not see him, squatting by the road; the car remained a closed shape in the half-dark. The road, the surface, on which he had leaned with one hand when he fell over, the grayness of flattened grit, the smell of asphalt—it had been sharp to the touch, uneven, a bad road, inlets of sand where it should have been paved, soft shoulders, *cuestas irregulares.*

Woods, darkly massed. Snow? Yes, but higher up, not where they were driving. Bare, snow-covered slopes, far away. Conifers, like an army. And mountains, not very high, ever more distant, hazy, each successive range more faintly outlined. No food, he had had no food. Only a sip from a drinking flask, lukewarm and bitter. Then more vomiting. And sleep. Dreams, Lucia, but very far away, unreachable. The man who had given him the piece of paper, he had been there when he had got into the car, mocking, holding himself aloof. The older man, asleep. Or not, but with closed eyes. Old, could have been an actor. In the theatre he had had big gleaming eyes, now closed. And she, immobile, a doll, had looked at him once, as though high up in the trapeze, before the leap. The look measuring the distance, the difference between falling and catching.

A plain, then more woods. The road flowing onward all by itself, seeking the depths of the valley, the softest parts of the hills, the natural track of animals before there was a road, the place of each bend a necessity of nature, the road climbing over itself, passing itself, like a snake. The road seeks the river becomes a bridge becomes a road. Shape of the man at the wheel. Black shoulders, black neck, hands on the wheel, lit-up dashboard, hood, and then again the road, running in the other direction, the one from which they have come, narrow in the distance, broadening, flowing past on both sides, making a sound. Then asleep again, sound of geese? Sound of geese, then no longer the sound of the engine, or only softly.

Voices. His language, yet not his language. Different music. Scornful, that is meant for him, about him, he knows. Gravel, doors, corridors, then nothing more, no one with him. He measures the room with his eyes. Tall, with two large windows. He hears shouts, then another voice, calling, a shot, more shouting. Silence, footsteps, sleep. He tries to think of Lucia, but however far he stretches out his arm, the thought of her recedes. It is not his arm. Now he would like to think of himself, but he cannot. When he tries again, there is a different light, no, there is a light. A plate of fruit stands beside him and a glass of water. He wants to sit up. The room begins to whirl. He closes his eyes and when he opens them again he looks fixedly at the fruit. They lie there very still. Slowly, oh how slowly, he reaches out his hand and follows that strange tool on its way to the biggest fruit, an apple. Behind it something shimmers and he sees, at the far end of his vision, beyond the back of his hand, beyond the fruit, a knee. His gaze rises as if he is being lifted up, and meets that of the old man. His eyes are not unfriendly; there is something like compassion in them.

13

Lucia stands in the doorway; the old woman has turned around and sees the panic in her face.

"What's the matter, can I help you?"

"My husband has gone."

The old woman knows at once that Kai has not just gone for a moment, but is gone. There is a kind of calamity that is immediately obvious: plain, stark fate. She gets up, takes Lucia by the hand and walks through the corridors with her, out of the building. The black car has gone. Kai and Lucia's is still there, its tires slashed. The clown takes her back into the building, gives her something to drink.

"What am I to do? I must warn the police."

"Better not. Was it that woman?"

Lucia nods.

"They call her the Snow Queen."

Lucia repeats the name. The strange words linger in the stuffy dressing room, among the clown's masks, the empty shoes. They emanate a threat. She repeats them once more, in disbelief and rage, stands up and says she must do *something*.

"We are going to do something."

"Why has she taken him away?"

Just by looking at the old woman she feels calmer. The clown has a broad face in which a strange serenity is garnered, a great store of wisdom. Serenity, wisdom, these are mere words. This woman is strong.

"Why?"

"Because she wanted to. She is very powerful in the part of the country where she lives. She doesn't come here often, but everyone knows her. They say it's a gang of robbers. In a castle, somewhere in the East, in the woods. We're sure to find it."

"A gang of robbers! I don't believe in fairy tales."

"That's wrong of you."

"What is?"

"Not to believe in fairy tales."

"Why?"

"Because many things can be explained through fairy tales."

The fairy tale is a fungus on reality. Travesty, apology, fungus, disease, caricature. The clown thinks all these things, more or less simultaneously, and says nothing. She hates fairy tales, but that is no reason not to believe in them. I will come back to that later.

Lucia looks at the old fat woman in front of her. "Abducted," she says softly, as if thereby to cast a spell over the moment.

As for me, here in Zaragoza, I had promised to keep out of it, but of course I cannot. Fairy tale, travesty, apology—I understand what she means, but I would never

61

have expressed it that way. Actually, she did not say it. I'm not crazy. But if someone asked me? That would cost me a kilometer. If I don't know the answer to something, I walk up and down the classroom and smoke. Ducados, but I don't inhale, or I would have been dead long ago. Ten Ducados is one kilometer. Don't ask me how I worked that out, even though I do know the answer. In fact, I can be very accurate in these matters. How can you start a story with "Once upon a time there was" if you don't know the answer? Dutch always helps me; it is an inspired language. *Sprookje,* tale, that which is told, told in language. Put into speech, therefore. *Spraec,* they say in the South, where Kai and Lucia are now, and there it means simply what someone *says,* his language, his words, his speech. *Spraec,* speech, speaking, spoken words, words told, a tale—and I have seen them there, in the marketplaces, the *spraec* speakers, for that is what they are called. But all right, all words acquire and lose meanings, and a fairy tale now means something which you still tell but which is not true because it cannot be true. What is true, and when? A man with an artificial heart is the subject of a tale told by Hoffmann, though it is called an *Erzählung.* And a man on the moon? That was not possible five hundred years ago, but in those days it was commonplace for a pope to be murdered. The pope with the smile, that is the sickening nickname they devised for the man who was allowed to be pope for only thirty-three days, as many days as Christ lived years. After that, he was murdered, or is that a fairy tale?

The tales of that time are the reality of today, and vice versa. So this is not getting me any further. What is a fairy tale? An intensified form of story, while a story is, or ought to be, not a copy but an intensified form of reality, history torn out of its slow chronology. Take Andersen, who usually starts off with a bang: "Listen to this!" Of course I would love to talk to the clown about the difference between story, reality and tale, but that is impossible, because she is in it, in the tale. And I am not, although sometimes it looks as if I am. Tales do not get interrupted, Tiburón, especially not by the person who tells them. There you are again, just as at the Colegio, long ago. "Where are you, Tiburón? Gentlemen, what you see there sitting at that desk is the bodily presence of our friend Tiburón, but his mind is elsewhere." Scornful laughter, but I was used to that. It is a miracle I ever got into Delft. There they used to think I rambled—I liked that word when at last I understood it—that I spent too much time on sidetracks, and me a budding road engineer! And yet, what did I once read about Diderot? "The art of digression is the intuitive approach to the complexity of reality." But what is reality, and besides, I am not Diderot. No, I have not solved the problem yet.

"We're off," said the old woman, coming toward Lucia. "We are going to look for him, and we shall find him. Take off that fancy dress, pack your cases, collect your wages and don't say anything to the manager, because he is a brute and a fool; and if you ask me, he knows what's going on, but he prefers not to get mixed up in anything. Fear is currenter here than money."

Currenter, currenter, thought Lucia, who found this a very strange word.

"Off we go," the clown said with sudden sternness, and she wanted to put her arm around Lucia's shoulder because she felt sorry for the girl. But Lucia was too tall, and clowns do, after all, exist by the grace of their imperfections. When they both stood up straight, the woman with the broad face did not even reach Lucia's shoulder blades.

"Off we go," she said again. "We're going *royling*." *Royling*, yes, wandering. This clown had many times crawled after her big yellow ball in the theatres of the South.

14

KAI had three questions for the old man who looked at him with such kindness. Where he was, why, and when he could leave. He received answers, too. He was in the castle that they called the hotel, he was with the Snow Queen, and when she no longer needed him, he could go.

"This isn't a hotel," said Kai.

"No, that is correct," said the man, who told Kai his name was Ulrich.

"Ulrich," said Kai, "no one can be called Snow Queen."

"You can if that's what people call you." This could not be denied.

"Why do they?"

"Because it's what she looks like."

"Ice Queen would have been better."

Ulrich sighed.

"Where is Lucia?"

"She's all right."

It sounded like a lie. The door opened, and the young man who had given Kai the piece of paper came in. He stroked Ulrich's hair and said, "Good morning, Papa."

"Good morning, Floris."

"Has he asked yet where he is, why he is here and how long he has to stay?"

"Yes."

"Exactly what I asked, too. Oh God, he's still wearing his fancy dress. What did you tell him? We're a gang, we live by smuggling and extortion, by corruption, deceit and the betrayal of others, and you'll never get out of here again except feet first? Watch it! Defection is punishable by death, and affection is why you are here. She'd already spotted you when you were standing by the roadside, and in the theatre there was no holding her."

He looked at Kai.

"Did he tell you that? I bet he didn't. You're a man with a future. Now you will never need to con stupid peasants again. I'm your predecessor; therefore, I do not like you. Ulrich is my predecessor; therefore, he does not like me. But Ulrich is old, aren't you, Ulrich? Old and discarded, but still used for advice. Always against everything. Against this, too, but not in order to please me. Why were you against it, Ulrich? Moved by the sight of golden hair and young happiness? I don't really speak their cesspool language, but Ulrich very easily gets *reweful*. He takes pity on people, we would say. That sounds nice, too. But Ulrich is *reweful*."

Kai tries to raise himself.

"Why am I here?" he asked. The two faces melted together, and he felt himself being pressed back into the bed again. The one face that the two had merged into became a mobile mask. It expressed a variety of emotions all at once: hatred, suspicion, jealousy, pity. But when it spoke, the voice was only Floris'.

"Asking the same question twice is stupid. You are here in order to please. After six months you'll be *horefodor,* just like me. Then you will be unrecognizable to your respectable self."

Kai has not heard the words, only the sound of his voice, which pulls him away to a place where he doesn't want to be. He asks once more why he is here.

"Do you always know why you are somewhere? I am here too, aren't I?" He strokes Kai's hair. Kai turns his head and sees the room swaying.

"I wouldn't worry myself about it. If you were five kilometers this way or that, you wouldn't know it either. You're here because you're so beautiful."

The masks break apart. The pitying one bends forward; the mocking one leaps up so suddenly that Kai can no longer see it.

"It's all going to be all right," says Ulrich.

"Stop being *reweful,* Ulrich; it's not going to be all right. This is hell to the third degree, and we're never going to get out of it, and he isn't either. For remember, you wizard," and then the bitter face is suddenly near him again, "you can't do anything just now, but when our love potion has worn off, don't you dare try to escape or we'll slit your throat with this."

The knife, short, curved, gleaming and razor sharp, hangs above him, motionless. Kai closes his eyes.

"And when are we allowed to wash him? He smells like a *ciboul.*"

Then there is another voice. When he hears the first

67

words, it sounds as if glass is breaking, loose fragments falling on stone.

"Let him sleep."

What remains is the tone. The separate words vanish; only the sound lingers, high and strange, as if someone were running a moist finger along the rim of a glass.

15

THE night that Kai cannot remember has been chiseled into Lucia's mind. There is a sound as of stone on stone in that word, and no wonder. Memory is not always a soft mass flowing apart. The clown's car looked like a hooded wagon; the only thing lacking was a horse, but one could not be sure whether perhaps the engine wasn't an animal. She had to talk to it in order to make it start. Later Lucia wondered how the old woman knew where she was going, and it was as well that the thought did not come to her at the time, because the clown had no idea. The East—more than that she did not know.

In the back of the vehicle lay a mattress, and beside it wobbled the suitcase with the shoes and the checkered suit in it; the yellow ball rolled pointlessly back and forth. With the addition of Kai and Lucia's luggage the car was very full and labored uphill.

It was quiet outside: there was hardly any traffic. Sometimes they saw the moon and a cohort of stars; then again swift, long dark clouds chased across the sky, hurrying to get somewhere. Different clouds, thought

Lucia, of a younger and more agile kind than the ones she was used to. Their quick passage cast receding shadows on the landscape, rocks seemed to fall slowly across the road, tall trees slanted threateningly above the car— all the things among which they moved were themselves in movement. Later in the night, when the moon showed them a clearing, they stopped. The old woman must have known the place, for she drove the car behind some bushes, so that they could not be seen from the road. Now at last it was really still: the total, absolute stillness that comes with the absence of other people and that therefore suggests the idea of your own absence, so that it seems as if perhaps you do not really exist at all.

So still it must also have been before there were any people, thought Lucia. The old woman had lit an oil lamp and brought out bread and cheese, and they had eaten in silence. Then the woman had gone away and Lucia had heard her urinate, but it was not so much the actions that were strange as the silence that returned after each action, intensified by the unfamiliar and unexpected sounds; for to someone who has always lived in the city, silence is reinforced by such sounds, despite the fact that they are sounds.

"Come, we'll go to sleep," said the clown. They got out of the car and climbed into the back.

"You needn't be afraid of anything."

She knew that Lucia was now thinking of Kai, but strange though it might seem, she was mistaken. Lucia tried, but couldn't. This was the first time in many years that she was about to spend a night without him. It felt like pain; something was missing from her, and the thought that belonged to the missing part refused to be recalled. She simply could not imagine where he was now and what he was thinking, and at the same time any picture she might have formed of him vanished from her thoughts. He was not there; the silence and the darkness did not yield him up. It seemed to her as though the woman beside her was very big and round, something consisting of warmth and breath, the breath of someone sleeping. Very peaceful, as if her new friend were linked to the sea and therefore part of a much larger, indefinable movement.

Most people do not know what the world is, but whatever else it is, it is also a clock. Here in Zaragoza it is evening, too. What follows next can be skipped; the story will continue later. It is not my custom to work in the evenings, but today I had no choice; it was almost forty degrees. Just now I went out onto the terrace on the school roof. Usually you cannot see the stars that well in the city, but this evening I saw them very clearly, the same stars that Lucia can see through the car's dirty rear window when she opens her eyes and there are no clouds. It is as well that she does not know what I know, that there are more stars than there are grains of sand on all the beaches of the world combined, and that many of these stars have their own planets. It would have frightened her, like the call of an owl, for she does not know what that is. It sounds like the voice of someone lost and wandering. Rustlings, branches snapping, but the breathing beside her continues calmly. At last she falls asleep, and now it is as if my book is also asleep. Perhaps I am afraid of that; it sighs and breathes softly on the table in front of me; it swells gently and then subsides again, just like the two women on their mattress side by side in the dark forest, just like unconscious Kai, abducted in a Tatra. Only *I* am awake. Perhaps there aren't any readers, so I'll just

71

do what I like for a while. Of course, I ought to be more severe with myself, but the night makes one weak. Besides, who reads my books? No one knows me in Spain, and even if my publisher accepts them, it is never more than a pitifully small edition.

I don't mind. I like writing but I don't want to live as a writer. I don't know how to put it. I don't believe in leaving traces; I believe only in the sort of fumbling which, even as a boy, I used to call thinking, though it had nothing to do with thinking and, at its best, only to do with meditating. Being printed equals being permitted to think aloud. The tale as an intensification of reality? But reality is such a muddy concept. If the road is reality, then what is the dream of a person in a car on that road? Everything starts with us and comes back to us, and in that sense the dream is as real as the hole in the road that shakes you out of your dream; but what is a hole other than something which is not?

Writing consists of always asking the same questions, and philosophizing seems to consist of always giving different answers. What does someone do when he writes a fairy tale? He takes the easy way out: he doesn't intensify reality; he distorts it; he makes it do things it cannot do. So he does not ask questions; he only gives answers, wrong answers that cannot be true, and in doing so he violates reality, and that is its intensification. A fairy tale must therefore be read with all-too-wide-open eyes. It is, after all, possible that distortions may make something clear about *form*. But what reality is, that I have not yet figured out, and that is why I never have the desire to copy it: let others do that, everyone has his own reality after all. Whether you are talking about colors or about the passing of time, it is always just you yourself speaking. Nothing fits together, that much I have learned from Spinoza and Hume, and this isn't meant to be name dropping; it's walking with a stick. All Spaniards do it. That is why we only have derivative philosophers, no real ones. Nothing fits; we are real and at the same time we want to say what reality is, like a shadow talking to its shadow.

Is that a marten by the car, a fox? A rustling around the rising and falling breath of the two women. The death screech of a small animal, a trail among the leaves, all those things they no longer know about in the North but which I still know with my half-empty packet of Ducados and my half-finished thoughts. The car stands like a church with its back toward the East. The first light peels the darkness from those two faces, shines on Lucia's closed eyelids. "I don't believe in fairy tales," she said. Someone ought to explain to her that if you look like her you are bound to end up in a fairy tale. Perfect beauty is also a distortion of reality, and therefore a form of fate. My old friend Webster, who is all I have here, has it. *Fairy tale, a tale relating to fairies. Fairy, fata,* literally *afate,* from the Latin *fatum,* fate. Does this carry me any further or does it leave me where I am? *An imaginary being in human form.* Three women, three fairies? Two good, one bad?

Suddenly Lucia sits up and lets out a scream. Apparitions of mist, veils, strands, white and grey, with hands and faces, creep, hover past the car window. She feels the woman's hand stroking hers and looks into a face that sees the same things as she, but smiles.

"What are they?"

"They are the dreams of other people." She laughs.

73

"Look," she says, "it's this," and she gets up with amazing nimbleness and runs her fingers through the leaves outside until her hands are wet, and rubs her face with them.

Lucia looks at the strands of mist that wind themselves around the trees, and she also runs her hands through the grass.

"They are on their way home and are leaving water for us," says the clown, and laughs.

16

HE HAS awakened again. This time there is no one. He raises his hand, which now moves normally through the air. His crazy headache has gone. It is day; cold light enters, marks out the room, tall and empty. He gets up, slowly, master of his own body once again, and goes to one of the large windows. He cannot hear his footsteps on the thick carpet, nor are there any other sounds. Everything seems deserted. From the window he sees another wing of the building in which he is held and which must be very large; a paved yard; a closed door in a blank wall; a wood beyond, half-bare, some of the branches still bearing drab, dirty yellow leaves. No movement behind the windows of the other wing. He thinks of Lucia, says her name aloud, and startles at the sound. Then he says it more softly, but it ought to call forth the person that belongs to it, and she refuses to appear. He walks cautiously around the room, sees his image in the mirror, walks past it, returns, and inspects himself. It looks like him. When he moves his hand, the other does the same. These things are very ordinary; only it has never happened to him before. So that is me, he thinks, and because he sees in the mirror what he is wearing, he looks down at his legs and arms and sees his theatre clothes, which have now become ridiculous. Hastily and ashamedly he takes them off. Beside the mirror is a door, half-open. Carefully he goes to it. It leads to a bathroom. He does not enter just yet, but first tries the other door of the room in which he has slept. This door is locked, but that does not frighten him; on the contrary, he is glad of it, as he is also glad of the silence and the absence of thoughts. As if he were about to bathe another person, that is how he feels. And that other person, he thinks, has a pain in his eye. He runs the bath, sniffs at a flask on the edge of the tub, and pours some of the honey-colored liquid into the water. Then he steps into the bath. When he is lying down, he makes waves with his hands, as if he thought he might then be able to float. He does not get out of the bath until a long time later, dries himself with a large towel that hangs there, re-enters the bedroom. The light has grown a fraction more somber. On the table by the bed there is a plate of cheese and fruit. At first he thinks it is strange to eat while naked; then he sits down on the bed and eats. When he has finished everything, he hears, as though someone had been waiting for this, the click of the door lock. He does not look up; he already knows. He feels the so-cool hands on his shoulders, feels how the nails press a cross in the flesh on his back, follows the command of one single finger, turning him around like a thing that can be turned around, and placing him opposite her, who is as tall as he. Her eyes survey him as they would a map, and her hands, no, her fingers, follow. They explore curves, bends, knots of muscles, hollows. The length of his fingers, the spaces between them, the

76

surface of his nails. All this time it is as though he does not see her. The fingers and the eyes travel independently; they meet, take leave, give way, make encompassing movements, come to a halt. It is as if he had never had a body before. The light recedes ever further from the room. Sometimes nothing happens for a long time; then a slight movement forces him backward, to one side; his arm is lifted, his neck bent. And then, as if the natural boundaries of the inspection have been reached without his comprehension, he suddenly finds himself lying down with her in his arms. She is fragile and made of the hardest glass, and as she chases him so he chases her, something in her, something that ought to be accompanied by loud cries, but he knows this must not be; everything takes place in an unbreakable silence of glass, and yet at the end it seems as if she breaks, snaps like glass, dies.

Only, there is no end—this breaking brings about a repetition, the soundless tone higher now, the breaking sharper, as if soon, when they get up, he will have to be careful not to tread on the fragments. His body changes more and more into something he does not know, something that exists only for itself, to which no thoughts belong, something that labors and cannot tire, any more than real objects can, any more than she can. What it produces is desire, but this is a product which devours itself the moment it is born, so that the ever-darkening room becomes ever colder, until it seems as if his new body has been hollowed out with a knife, as if every secret corner, every spot hitherto thought insignificant, has been leached and wrung dry and he is left prostrate, as empty as a sloughed skin. She raises herself above him and for the first time he sees her, whom he has seen a

77

thousand times this afternoon, gliding by, absent, chasing, escaping, compelling, like a real being, yet as emptied as he, and still closed and inaccessible. It has been no use, he thinks; only slaughter and breaking can avail here; but she says, as she sits up, a luminous, hardened figure in the dark: "We are *sibbet.*"

"*Sibbet*?"

He does not understand her. Now it really does seem for a brief moment as if she is laughing. She moves her left forefinger, then the right, and hooks the two into each other, and pulls, as if it would be impossible to separate them.

"*Sibbet,*" she says, and vanishes, as soundlessly as she had come.

He waits for the soft click of the lock that leaves him alone again.

17

IT WAS morning. The mists had gone, taking away their spirits. Like all people waking up in strange surroundings, Lucia began to add the world up, and as this cannot really be done—the cold and the hand of the person sleeping beside you and the trees outside the car window and the last thoughts before you fell asleep—the addition sum becomes as long as the visible world itself, and then the things you cannot see have to be added as well. But this is how it appeared: tall treetops outside the two small windows, the blue sky, the clown's big yellow ball, the clown herself, who now, waking up in the daylight, had blue eyes that looked at Lucia calmly and kindly. She pulled the blanket away from them both, opened the car door, stepped onto the grass, hummed and, exactly as on the night before, ran her hands through the leaves and the grass and rubbed the cool clear water over her face, and Lucia did the same.

It was still very cold, but they made a few dancing steps, sang a little and listened to the reply of the birds, shook the branches and called it a shower, and sat in the open rear doors of the car to have something to eat. Lucia, who was still supposed to be sad, was indeed sad, though not as sad as she had expected. There was another feeling, which should not be named, which belonged more to the bustle of the birds, to the crazy dancing steps she had just taken, and to the woman who was sitting there so contentedly, letting a thick stream of golden honey pour onto her bread.

They really ought to have been setting off now to look for Kai, but Lucia's new friend seemed to think that each day was allowed to remain as empty as the sky above their heads, and pottered about in the car.

"I can always feel if there's water nearby," she said, "Come along, you carry this." And she gave Lucia two long pieces of wood which, together with the thinner sticks she herself was carrying, would form a fishing rod when they reached the water.

The sun was climbing slowly; patches of light fell among the dead leaves. A snake, a squirrel, a badger, a hare, a wild boar, a beetle—everything took to its heels and watched from the bushes to see what would happen next. Overhead, two crows appeared, conducting a dignified though grumpy conversation while flying around in fanlike circles and watching the two women make one stick out of five, sit down on a large tree trunk by a lake and, within an hour, fetch up four gleaming, squirming trout from the water.

Then the two women told each other the stories of their lives, and of course the crows understood nothing of it, apart from noticing that the old woman's story was very short and the young woman's very long. These are laws that everyone who has lived a little longer knows. The longer life knows the joylessness of enumeration and avoids it. It knows that there are never more than a few things that determine someone's life. So Lucia learned that the clown, whose name was Anna, had once been a famous actress in the North. She also mentioned her other name and saw that it evoked an echo in Lucia, that the name still wandered about the North, which she had left so long ago, as a mere name, separated from the fat woman she had become. That name belonged to the roles she had played, which no one would ever see her play again. Actors leave nothing with their former audiences except a memory. When the memory dies, names linger like empty things, uncontrolled and without associations. Anna had long since resigned herself to this. Something had happened in her life that had led her to leave at the height of her fame. She had now become an old foolish man with a yellow ball, and she enjoyed it. She did not tell Lucia half of all this, but listened attentively to the stories about the trapeze, the circus, Reier and Kai. Two women eating fish in a forest, that was how it looked; and if anyone had been there to watch, he might not have dared to come closer. Old age and beauty—it was like an allegory.

"And now?" asked Lucia, as if she had forgotten where they were going.

"Over there," said Anna, pointing to the east.

When they drove off, Lucia looked back at the empty clearing and reflected that she would not have minded staying longer. But this was a forbidden thought. They drove along the same road Kai had taken, which I, because I have something to do with roads, would have been happy to describe, especially beyond the point where it forked and Anna took the wrong turning. However, they still continued in an easterly direction, so it did not matter very much. Occasionally, at one of the scarce filling stations—some of which, unlike in the North, looked like cozy little village squares because there were always clusters of people hanging around—Anna asked something in the language Lucia could only barely understand; but it seemed as if the answers were always different. A day and a night, and the same again.

Now they are sleeping by a waterfall, beside a deep cave into which, at sunset, large numbers of pigeons fly, just as at the Monasterio de Piedra some hundred kilometers south of Zaragoza. The pigeons skim past the cascading water and find a resting place in the cave. They potter about for a while, wings beating, and then go to sleep. Lucia has never really thought much about living things and is filled with wonder. More and more pigeons arrive, until it looks as though the walls of the cave are feathered and alive. She looks at the thundering, transparent sheet of water crashing onto the rocks beneath, as it has perhaps done uninterruptedly for thousands of years. She wants to think something but cannot.

"Don't look too long," says Anna, who has made a fire. "It makes you sad."

Then they hear, not very far away, the sound of voices, men and women, voices that talk and sing, laughter.

Lucia wants to get up; Anna holds her back.

"Those are the Screemers," she says, but before she has time to explain, it is as if the sound has turned a corner and is suddenly very close. Laughter, something like drums and bells. It sounds cheerful, not frightening. The women's voices answer the men's, the high and the low sounds follow one another like waves, and each wave sounds like an invitation. Lucia sways to the rhythm.

"Can't we go and look?" asked Lucia.

"*Sely goose,*" said Anna, and for a moment she looked, even without her mask, like the clown from the circus.

"You don't need to go and look; they'll soon be here."

18

THE *autopista* is not within my competence. No, let me first sound a warning. This is a chapter I reserve altogether for myself. At the beginning of *Henri Brulard* Stendhal talks of all those odious *I*'s and *Me*'s that are so embarrassing and intrusive. I agree with him. But the third person is in such cases a shabby circumvention, as if there existed a country somewhere inhabited only by Third Persons who can be summoned by proclamation to carry out brotherly services for you when you are temporarily overcome by shame. After all, you think of so many things while you are writing, and what would be the use of that if it all had to stay outside the book. Imagine this literally. Take this book, if it ever becomes a book, for if it doesn't the problem does not arise. But all right, take this book and place it upright in front of you on the table, facing away from you, with its back toward you. Admit that it is an odd object. Now feel with your hand the empty space to the right and left of the book, and of course, you feel nothing. Yet I always think there must be something. Close to the cover are the thoughts the writer had while he was writing but which he did not allow to get into the book. Writing is a question of organization and therefore of taking decisions, and among these decisions are what will be in a book and what will not and when it will be finished. What I am doing here is strange, but once begun, it isn't easy to stop. When you look at the yellow Michelin map number 43, you see the *autopista* that leads from Barcelona to the west, via Lérida—Lleida, the Catalonians say—to Zaragoza. This *autopista*, then, is not my responsibility. Thank God, for it is a road without a soul. Alongside it is the N 11. I don't care much for that either; if you ever use it you'll know why. My favorite road in that part of Aragón is the C 1130. It arrives rather confusingly as the C 231 from the south at Torrente de Cinca, then crosses the *autopista* and the N 11 and climbs up along the Rio Cinca. I always give it preferential treatment, although obviously I cannot take it out of my budget, for that would be noticed. It is more a question of attention. I will not now describe this road, or rather the landscape, in further detail; all I want to say is that I can always think better when I am there. There is little traffic on it, because the world is in a hurry and, at least if you want to go to Zaragoza, it is a roundabout way. *Desvia*, we say in Spanish, but I don't like that word much. The Dutch *omweg*, way around, sounds better. *Om* has a magic resonance, as if it is made of bronze; you can say it a hundred times and there are countries where they meditate on that word. Om, om, om.

Yesterday I suddenly couldn't stand it any longer in the classroom. I had become all the children at once; I had smoked twice my ration and was almost suffocating. Such a moment occurs in every book. It is the last attempt of the characters to escape existence and of the events to escape taking place. People underestimate what it is, to happen, and yet not to happen in reality. Anyway, I saw the familiar shape of my Seat standing in the school yard, with that languid good-naturedness of objects waiting until they can be of service to you.

At Sariñena the C 1130 changes into the C 129. There is a logic in these numberings, but it is not of my invention. When you drive along the C 129 in the direction of Zaragoza, you can, after Leciñena, take an even smaller road that runs alongside the Rio Gallego to Zaragoza and has no number on the Michelin 43. This little road leads to a Carthusian monastery, the Cartuja de Aula Dei. There aren't many of those left. It is the strictest order there is: the monks live in isolation even within the monastery, receiving their food through a hatch and assembling only a few times a week for sung prayers and, strangely, for a walk. I like it there. I come from a more or less anarchistic family, and the monks know I am not religious, but they don't mind; God knows, maybe they pray for me. When I am there, the door of the world shuts behind me. I chat a little with the guest-padre. The others you don't get to see, and anyway they're not allowed to talk, not even among themselves. Afterward I usually sit for a while in the monastery church, which is fairly ugly and contains a few dull early Goyas. It is cool in that church, and this is a blessing in the province of Zaragoza, which is more like the Sahara than like Europe. So I sit there, thinking of this and that, and after a while I go away again and take with me a jar of honey that the monks have made themselves. When I bring it home, my wife always gives me a look of "so that's how the wind blows." Although I may be wrong, maybe she knows in advance that I am going there. I'd rather not probe into that too much.

So yesterday I walked, literally with thumping heart, to my car as if I were about to play truant, and so of course I was. I swept out of town and onto the *autopista,* for I wanted to take my favorite road and approach the Cartuja by a roundabout route. That way I would have two meditations, one while driving and one in the church.

A person like me must be very careful on the *autopista,* for there is little traffic and, before you know where you are, you lose yourself in daydreams. After all, unlike other road users, I do not drive through one landscape, but two, one of which is in my head. Here it was summer; there it is winter. And when I was not paying attention, I saw the miserable mountain roads of the Southern Netherlands running across the indolent dual lanes of the *autopista.* At Torrente de Cinca I turned off and took the C 1130 to Ballobar. To my right flowed the Cinca, if you can call it flowing, for it was more like the trail of a tear on the cheek of a dead body. The landscape is majestic here. Huge loam-colored altars stand in the plain as if a race of giants once lived here that worshiped a god as big as a mountain. Nothing grows; what people do here is simply a mystery to me. They scratch about in the earth and always manage to come home with something, and for the rest I believe they make sausages. Not many people live here, though. This road of mine is a mere luxury.

I have sometimes tried to translate the Dutch expression *wie schetst mijn verbazing* to my friends: who sketches my surprise? The Spanish with their literal minds always imagine someone with a sketchbook. But my surprise at what I saw on my road today defied all description: a girl hitchhiker from Zeeland, about twenty-five years old, suntanned, fair-haired and beautiful. She had a little Dutch flag on her rucksack and behaved as if it were the most natural thing in the world for her to be standing there. The temperature was over thirty-seven degrees yesterday, and suddenly there were two smooth brown legs beside me in the place that had been empty a moment before. She came from Sas van Gent, and what she spoke was almost Flemish. I love that, especially when it is spoken by women with not too high a voice; then it has something fibrous, at once soft and rough, caused by the slight aspiration, by the way air is added to the words. Real Flemish, as they speak it among themselves. I cannot always understand, but her I understood very well; and that harsh, naked sound that Northern Dutch has—as if every adornment were a superfluity and would detract from the certainty of the assertions—she did not have. She didn't seem surprised that I, a Spaniard, spoke Dutch, although she did laugh at my accent at times, and indeed, why not?

She had come from the coast, where she had taken part in that latter-day annual ritual, the resurrection of the dead. I went to look at it once. From all over Europe they come, the white bodies, as if the Last Trumpet had sounded. Nudist beaches are permitted here these days, but just as nakedness used to be a taboo in the past, so it is now forbidden to be white. All those bodies torment themselves during the day in order to stand before the mirror in the evening and, for these two weeks in the year, look invulnerable and therefore immortal. Everyone has his own resurrection. I do not say this out of prudishness, but I don't believe in it—it is a false faith, and during these rites they display their uninteresting genitalia to each other while at the same time pretending not to see them. Fatter or older people ought not to take part, but they do. They are not welcome; they disturb the illusion of paradise—the fat ones because they evoke thoughts of intemperance and therefore of the resulting Dantesque punishments of sickness, death and damnation; the old ones because they shamelessly display precisely that which everyone tries to deny, namely the future. They are like a silent but hysterical sect, all those nameless bodies that lie there burning like Saint Laurence on his roasting grid, as if they wished to be irradiated against the cancer of death or to anticipate their own cremation, whereby the body, as a punishment because it has betrayed them, is pulverized at high speed in a macro-oven, until not a trace of their nameless lives is left.

She laughed a little at my words, said I was a moralist, that I rambled on (there they were again, the magpie and the finch); and I suddenly felt unspeakably old. What then did I think I could offer her, the life of the spirit? I tried to see myself the way she saw me, and naturally, it started off with my inevitable blue suit, but I soon gave up, because I realized that she did not see me at all.

I asked if she had any objection to visiting the monastery with me, and explained to her what Carthusians were. She thought it a rather unbelievable story. It often strikes me about the younger generation that they know so little. She was a student of sociology and she had heard of monasteries, certainly, but no, she said, she had never realized it was that bad.

"But they don't think it's bad," I said.

"How do you know?" She used the familiar form of address. The formal mode has died out in the Netherlands, or almost, or else I still look younger than I thought, but I don't think so. And the question was a fair one.

"See for yourself," I said. "There's nothing like field work."

We turned into the drive leading to the monastery. On the left you see what looks like a curious factory with rows of little chimneys. The drive has a nineteenth-century air about it. Cool, shady plane trees, a faded photograph. There is something comfortable about it. I rang the bell, and after a long time I heard the guest-padre shuffling down the corridor. I had never been there with a woman before, or I would not have made such a fool of myself, for she was not allowed in. Father Anselm said it in a slightly apologetic but firm tone. He did not seem surprised at the tall, fair figure in shorts. She was allowed into the reception room, but women were not admitted to the rest of the monastery.

"Oh, cunt," she said.

"That is precisely what it is all about," I told her.

"No, it's because I'm wearing shorts. I had the same in the Vatican once. Bunch of dirty old men."

But it was more basic than that. She had hit the nail on the head with her first remark, though in the circumstances it may have been an infelicitous expression. However, I wanted to meditate in the church for a while. I am very attached to my habits.

It was half dark in the reception room. Against her will, that was obvious, she sat down in one of the hard armchairs and lit a cigarette. On the wall hung a hand-colored steel engraving of La Divina Pastora, at which she looked in disdain. I noticed for the first time how odd a picture it was. The Divine Shepherdess was sitting on an invisible seat and dressed in a pink gown whose clumsy folds covered her sturdy, not unattractive legs. Her not exactly straight eyes were raised heavenward, probably on account of the Divine Child that stood stiffly, in a yellow skirt, beside her. Her large flabby hand hung down on the child's chubby arm, which made one think of food. The child looked at nothing, not even at the lamb that leaped up at him eagerly, to reach the tiny fiery heart that was miraculously fixed to the outside of his body. The lamb sniffed at it, and perhaps would have liked to eat it, which is out of the question. But then the male figure with wings, walking through the sky, did not belong to the realm of the possible either. A second lamb sniffed at a rose pinned to the Mother's blue cloak, a third one knelt and nibbled, or so it seemed, at her pink toes. She was wearing a shepherdess' hat of the sort that, since Marie Antoinette, has been in fashion everywhere except among shepherdesses, and she was holding a curious staff. The whole party sat under a tree.

"It looks like some voodoo print," said the girl from Zeeland. "What does it all mean, for God's sake?"

Father Anselm smiled delicately when I translated what she said, and beckoned her to follow him to a small side room, where he opened a curtain. I thought I would be better off in the church now, though I probably wouldn't do much meditating.

To my surprise, I did.

Within minutes my book was standing all around me. There is always something uncanny about the as yet un- written—it pulls and sucks. It is like a kind of cramp. Unwritten, it wants to avenge itself; once written, that which was not there before creates a sort of stringy mel- ancholy, which wears off only very slowly.

Melancholy also troubled the girl from Zeeland; I could tell that when I returned. She was bending over a model of the monastery and gave me a shattered look, the look of rational people who are confronted with something that does not fit into their system. Usually it has to do with the fact that they think other people are letting themselves down. I knew this model quite well; it looked mostly like a doll's house, really, and since a monastery is a closed (*claustrum*) world, it was at the same time a portrayal of the universe. Everything was there, including the room we were in, which gives the impression that you exist twice. For her benefit I traced with my finger the route I had followed through the, to her, forbidden realm. She watched, but her mind was elsewhere, beyond the boundary that has remained closed also to me.

"Those aren't chimneys," she said vehemently, pointing at the strange little turrets you can see from the road. "They're watchtowers. They all have their own . . . what do you call them in Spanish?"

"*Miradores*. They all have their own *miradores*."

This seemed to agitate her. It seemed to express more poignantly than anything the grim, self-inflicted loneliness. She bent over one of the minute compartments, the cell of one monk. The cells were joined to each other, but without internal communication.

"Look, that's his bed. And here at the table he can sit and read."

It was correct. As in a real doll's house, a little manikin in a black and white habit was sitting by a table reading a book smaller than the nail of your little finger.

"And there he can pace up and down." She pointed to the passage behind the cell that could scarcely be longer than three meters.

"And then he goes upstairs, here, behind his lavatory, there are the stairs, to his . . . *mirador*. Then he can look out into the distance. And through this hatch he gets his food."

Her voice had acquired something plaintive; her blonde

hair hung over the turret—hair that none of the monks, except Anselm, would ever see. I wondered what it would be like to pace up and down in that passage, like a wolf, and climb the stairs to watch out over the sandy plain, like Moses in the desert. But as usual I could not imagine how it would be. Like a wolf? In a zoo you sometimes see them as if they're on a chain. The most sinister thing is always that skittish, neurotic sideways lurch with which they turn before starting the next loop. But monks don't walk like wolves. They take an hour over three meters and think thoughts from beyond this world. Or do they?

I bought my honey and we left. When we were a few hundred meters from the monastery, she suddenly said, "Stop the car a minute."

I stopped. She turned in her seat so that her safety belt stretched tightly across her breasts, and she looked at the row of *miradores* that kept watch over the plane trees like dead soldiers.

"Their whole life," her voice leaped, "they sit there, and all because of a fairy tale!" The word was uttered with the greatest contempt.

"It isn't a fairy tale; it's a faith."

"Nonsense. That voodoo print, I suppose, that child with his heart on the outside, and that mother with a white sun around her head."

She was referring to the halo of the Virgin Mother.

"Virgin Mother!" She spat that out also. "They're mad. It's slow suicide. People don't have the right to punish themselves like that. For a fairy tale!" She had said it again.

Faith, fairy tale, myth. I thought of the clown and at the same time of Robert Graves, the way one sometimes does. He once wrote an introduction to the *Larousse Encyclopedia of World Mythology*. Myths are to us so strange that we cannot believe they are true, because they have to explain something that cannot be true, he wrote— or words to that effect—adding, with a fantastical lyrical leap, that *therefore* the Bible stories, however much they may resemble Persian or Babylonian myths, do not occur in the standard works on mythology, simply because there are still people who believe in them. As soon as the last believer is dead, a religion becomes a myth, that's what it boils down to. Mary was immaculately conceived, she was a virgin when Christ was born, Christ was the son of God, after their deaths he and Mary were taken bodily to heaven and we will all rise from the dead to be judged.

The men who sometimes stood on those turrets believed all this, and that was why for the time being it was not yet included in the *Larousse Encyclopedia of World Mythology,* for no one dares put it in. We knew those men believed in a myth, and they were convinced they didn't. Fairy tales had nothing to do with it. Fairy tales are written by people—that is what is wrong with them. Myths are washed up, written by no one, and only later written down.

"Fairy tales are things that aren't true. I don't like fairy tales."

I felt her stamping her feet, and swerved to avoid a donkey.

Perhaps in some mysterious way myths were invented by all of us together. But why should someone write fairy tales? Because reality is unbearable? Myths were not written by anyone—it must have something to do with that. The writing of fairy tales is a false longing for the writing of myths, and therefore a longing to be no one, or to be a whole people, a mass without name or face, a vanished species. But it was too late for that.

When you approach it from the north, the skyline of Zaragoza is one of the most beautiful in Spain. You see the towers of the Seo and the Lonja on the other side of the Ebro; the city looks like a great mysterious ship sailing past in the desert.

"At least that's true," I said.

She put her slender hand on my arm, and it startled me.

"What's your name?" she asked. I told her.

"Tiburón." She pronounced it slowly.

"Does it mean anything?"

"Yes. It means shark."

I have always thought that the Dutch word for shark, *haai*, expresses better what a shark is than *tiburón*, which sounds more like a submarine.

"Shark. I don't think you're like a shark at all. What's your constellation?"

I didn't know. I don't believe in fairy tales, I wanted to say, but I didn't.

"Where are you going now?" I asked.

"To Pamplona, and then home."

Home! Suddenly I saw it: the ferry at Breskens; the wide, salty mouth of the Scheldt; the flat, fat, green land. She looked at me with those blue eyes as if she saw something that cannot be seen, something that is mine and that I always protect. I was standing by the Ebro and thought of the Scheldt, and it was as if I felt the wind of Scheldt, for I suddenly shuddered. Or so it seemed. "Why don't you take me there?"

Now I knew why I had shuddered. There she stood, the North. Yet I also had to be in that same country, but then in its backward, speechless, forgotten, fairy-tale part.

"I have work to do."

"I see." And she took hold of my Spanish engineer's head with both her hands, plonked two kisses on it and then a third one randomly, in the middle near my eyes, grabbed her rucksack from the backseat, said "bye-bye shark," and went away, a swinging blonde figure with the tan of the Mediterranean Sea, my sea, springily, without looking back, just as all the worst writers in the world would have it.

I drove back to the school, put my finger in the honey jar and licked long and pensively, and saw the long fair hair hanging into the monk's cell. I am not much of a shark. And this chapter has gone on for too long. On the other hand, among the Japanese, asymmetry is regarded as essential in aesthetics. At least one nation that does not believe in perfection. Or does it?

19

MEANWHILE, Kai had become a chauffeur. You might think this would have given him an opportunity to escape, but the thought did not cross his mind. He remembered all too well Floris' semicircular knife above his throat, and besides, on his journeys he felt like an actor in an American gangster film, preferably in black and white. He loved driving the big Tatra, even though the trips were never longer than a few hundred kilometers. Usually Floris sat beside him and gave a bitter running commentary on the landscape. They always seemed to have to collect something or other on these trips.

Floris or Ulrich or, on shorter journeys, one of the other men whose names no one had ever told him and whose speech he could barely understand, would enter a house somewhere and reappear shortly afterward. Kai never asked any questions, and no one told him anything. Sometimes there would be a great noise or a shattering of glass; sometimes he heard shots, and then he had to drive extra fast afterward; or, at Floris' direction, shake off a pursuer.

He did these things like a perfect automaton: he drove the car, and another, nameless agent drove him. What preoccupied him, but only occasionally, were the pain in his eye and the visits the woman paid to his room. All these things had come into his life since he had left the North. Different laws applied here. He did not call the woman by any name, and in any case, speech was not required of him. She was a circle closing ever more tightly around him. He was aware that in the castle, or hotel, as they called it, jokes were made about him, but he did not react. The only thing he observed in himself was a restlessness when she did not come, or when it seemed to him that she was late. Perhaps he had become addicted to those silent occurrences in which forms of pain and compulsion and pleasure were intermingled. A will that seemed bent on destruction and that was so much stronger than his ruled him in a way nothing had ever ruled him before. When it was over, he was left without memory—a person sitting on the edge of his bed in total silence or staring out of the window for hours.

Inside the castle he was free to go where he pleased, a privilege he made little use of. The place was mostly like a cross between a hotel, a boarding school and a prison, he thought, and most of the other inmates were not to his liking. Sometimes he chatted for a while with Ulrich, who was beginning to look more and more tired and who treated him like a child or like someone you can't take altogether seriously. There was a lot of gambling going on, whereby Floris, who one day turned up in a uniform from some stage performance and on the next day in a dinner jacket or another incongruous garment, behaved so provocatively that the game often ended in a fight and Ulrich had to intervene.

There were no women. He usually had his meals with Floris and Ulrich. She was never there, and he did not know where she had her rooms. On some days there were more men than usual. Then he preferred to stay in his room, from which he could hear music and drunken shouting. Once he saw someone being led bleeding out of a room by two others. Mortal fear, that was what he had seen in the man's eyes, but even then he had asked no questions. There was a veil between him and the rest of the world, and he lived behind it as in an aquarium. When he looked into her eyes—but this he did not like to do too often—he saw in them that she did not see him, as if what occurred between them did not really have anything to do with him and as if beside him there was another, impersonal force in the room, namely an all-consuming, voracious lust. There was nothing to be seen in those eyes. You looked into tunnels of glass and ice that led to a world where it was so cold that, if you penetrated too far into it, you would freeze to death.

20

Fairy tales are one-dimensional stories. That is why they can even have objects as their main characters, as you can see in Andersen. The fairy tale of the candles: "Once upon a time there was a large wax candle who knew her worth." The heroine is a candle and has only one character trait. Fairy tales are closed systems, that is what makes them so terrifying. "Down came the comet, blazing forth from its fiery center and with threatening tail," "The well was deep; that was why the rope was so long." Everything always tallies; a writer has nothing to seek there. The outcome is fixed, the characters have only one dimension, no lies can be told except in such a way that everyone notices it. Assignment: tell a story in the manner of a fairy tale of a terminal cancer case, with the greedy, proliferating cells as the wolves hungry for Little Red Ridinghood. Bet it will work? Forty degrees today.

21

"AH, *honyflode, honyseime,*" said the man with the gold-colored beard on whose lap Lucia was sitting; and he stroked her hair and her shoulders. She sat, no, lay, with her head thrown back and saw the clear light of autumn through the last leaves. When the branches moved, the rays of light shifted and seemed to be chasing one another, as if they wanted to intertwine. Around them there could be heard the clucking and murmuring of others, kisses, caresses, touches, the soft crackling of twigs and dead leaves under their writhing bodies. Sometimes a ray of light fell vertically. Then she looked up to see how his head was lit by that ray, and he saw it and smiled from his suddenly more radiant face and pretended to grasp the ray. He whispered "God" to the light and "God" as he touched her shoulder or her breasts and "God" while lifting up a leaf so that it assumed a golden glow and she could see its veins like a pen-and-ink drawing.

God. That was something she had never concerned herself with, but he said it so often and always with that hum in his voice, so that now, when she looked at water or at a bird, she, too, softly and cautiously, without moving her lips, muttered that odd, short word with which he sealed things. How long had this been so? She pulled a hair from his beard and wound it round her fingers, one coil for each day. So the thin, finely spun end was the first day, when the singing and the drums had sounded in the woods, and Anna had said "the Screemers," a name they had presumably acquired because they always made so much cheerful noise. Before she had had a chance to think about it, they were already standing close by, rocking and dancing, he in front, a straggling group of men and women and children, and they had greeted Anna and Lucia as if they had known them for a long time, and he had put his hand on their heads, and it had been as if a bird had alighted there. Then they had shared food and pitched their tents, and it had become quiet until evening fell and the singing and dancing started again and they had lit a great bonfire.

She unwound the hair and held it up in the sunlight. That was how much time had passed, but he did not believe in time. What it was, time, she had never really asked herself, and she did not need to, either, for he had said that time would cease. How that could be she did not know, but he had said it: the end of time. For when this century came to an end, a thousand years would have been completed and the few years that still remained were the last respite; after that, everything that existed in time would cease, together with time. She had seen Anna smile, though you might have thought it was a reason for sadness, but he and his friends did not seem to be troubled by it either. They clapped and danced while he kept repeating it, his voice higher and more insistent each time. Then they stood up and danced, arms on each other's shoulders, their faces filled with a strange joy. The end of the millennium, the three zeros, which he outlined in the darkening air, like circles above the fire—you would vanish into those zeros, depart, singing all the while, to a place where it was better, as if the holes in those zeros drawn in the air had a power of attraction so great that it would make everything disappear into them. In the absence of time, which would then follow, everything would dissolve, crumble, vanish, and what would be left would be no more than a sigh, the sigh itself, the memory of the sigh, and then nothing. Like the lions in the circus everyone would then leap through the fiery hoops of those three zeros, and he was the lion tamer.

Thousand, thousand, the word went whispering and shimmering among the small crowd, and she had felt Anna's arm about her and asked if it were true, and Anna had smiled and swayed to the rhythm with the others and said that thousand was only a man-made measure and that, whenever this number came near, some people felt a suction, a yearning, pulling them away from the constant counting, because counting reminded you of death, and such people, in their fear of dying, long for death, preferably together in a group. Lucia had not understood this, but then wine had been passed around, sweet and heavy, and he had danced around the fire like a madman so that it looked as if he were ablaze; and he had called out that God was in the fire and that everything was God and therefore the fire, too, and they themselves; and then he had held up his hands until they all fell silent, and he had pointed at the rents in his clothes, and they had all torn their clothes even further so that they were even more ragged than before; and in spite of the cold he had taken off his clothes and called out that, if everything were

God, then sin must also be part of God and that being part of God was good whether you were part of his light or his dark side, for to him light and dark, good and evil are the same, since in him there are no contradictions, and therefore, that which people called evil could never be contrary to good, for in a God who is one and indivisible there can be no contradictions; and then the voice coming from his golden mouth had begun to croon on an even higher note, and he had said that they were still being persecuted because they were the only free people in the world, that this world was doomed in which people of the same origins held others in possession and made them work like slaves and dictated how they should live, and that soon the scourge would come and put an end to all injustice in one huge purifying fire of destruction.

The scourge, the scourge—at this word it seemed as if his voice leaped above the trees and returned and struck, like a whip, the faces that looked at him in rapture; and after that his words were no longer intelligible because the sound he uttered seemed like one long, stammering note that swelled, time and time again, to a whiplash, while the voices of the others, equally high pitched, expressed the pain caused by the blows of the whip.

She thought later that she had been afraid of him then, yet at the same time excited, because his voice lifted her up and took her away and then, fortunately, brought her back again, becoming lower, calmer, until his words were once again distinguishable and he was no longer speaking of punishment but of love. Love, love—the word slithered away in all directions. It had to reach to the animals in their holes, the birds in their nests; it wanted to leap over the trees and vanish with the smoke of the fire into the sky, up to the stars, until it finally came down and settled in the gestures, in the hands with which they touched, caressed one another, still sighing and murmuring, swaying in the glow of the fire as if all of them together consisted of one large, mating body that did not feel the cold and could dance lying down until daybreak. But long before that time he had come to her, a figure of fire, and had held out his hand with a smile that spun her into a cocoon, the smile of a lion tamer who watches the lion leap through the perfect O of his burning hoop. She had looked back at Anna, who more than ever resembled a benevolent clown, and Anna, as if she had known about all this in advance, had nodded, expressing a great many things with this one movement; and then they had gone away from the circle around the fire and away from all the others, until the fire was merely a distant glow, and there he had loved her like a cloud.

A cloud? Yes, a cloud, something that was full and everywhere at once, a living cloud in the shape of a man with a gold-colored beard, the beard from which she had pulled the luminous hair she was now winding and unwinding around her finger as if she could wind time itself around her finger; and in the deception that belonged to this, it was as if her former life, her name and perhaps she herself were dissolved, flowing away in an element that belonged to nothing, where words did not count, where everything was as full and empty as a cloud that passes unhindered through the sky.

22

Now I am myself sitting on a lap, and what a lap. This seems a plebeian form of imagery and metaphoric delusion, like so much of what I do here, but how can you keep aloof when, amid the honeyed sounds of that Chrysostom, you hear another recalcitrant voice, whose ever more penetrating consonants rise to a roar, like the jammer of a pirate station just when you are listening to Mozart? And when that hateful intruding voice, which no one else can hear, is actually your own, raging more and more furiously until all harmonies are drowned, you might as well switch off Mozart altogether.

But I can't help it; I am allergic to the word *God*. I cannot hear it without my own voice countering it, cannot write it without my left hand at the same time trying to tear up the paper or starting to write independently, in a different, more obstinate fashion, sloping in a different direction, into another book. And why all the fuss? Do I myself not visit a monastery from time to time? True, but the Carthusians don't bother anyone; they want nothing from the world. I go there of my own accord; it does not, as it used to in the past, assail me without my having asked for it; it doesn't demand anything of me.

I ought to take a leaf out of Anna's book; women are always wiser. They know what I myself know: that the world has seen and digested many such millenarian fantasies before. The voluntary poor, the Ranters, the Fraticelli, the self-deification, the ravings of Plotinus, the brethren of the Free Spirit, whose reflection you meet again later, dressed up as science, in Spinoza, who identifies his impersonal God with Nature, heavenly goodness, and then, literally, always again that one same, all-embracing Blessedness in which everything, even the Trinity, would one day dissolve, the human soul seen as a drop fallen from the Divine horn into which it would be poured back after its transient, undivine life—all those doctrines with their hysterical belief in equality, inevitable component of the ever higher-surging waves of total deification, all those fantasies, the falsified decrees of the Pseudo-Isidore and his *Epistles of Pope Clement* that Clement never wrote, the egalitarian paradisal dreams of the *Roman de la Rose,* the right to happiness, the right to one another's bodies, splendid, seductive but mendacious rantings, endlessly reiterated utopian delusions with which mankind is deceived again and again!

Take any one of these half-baked Mediterranean pipe dreams and transfer it into the twentieth century when the zeros are on the march once again; take it to the jungles of Kampuchea and pay a visit to Pol Pot, in whose ideology no more property and no more cities are allowed to exist, no family and no sentiment, no music, no song, no books, no knowledge of the past. Three million people have died for that, because people always must die when a utopia is made law.

But at the start there is always seduction; there are always the men with the golden mouths, like that madman on whose lap Lucia now sits!

Lap, lap, stop it, Tiburón! You are alone. Keep calm. Here I am, in the middle of my classroom, my finger burned by the Ducados, like a monk pacing up and down his cell; when I look at the ceiling it is open and the golden hair of a giantess hangs down. I could climb it like Tarzan climbing up a liana! You are ranting again; you're mixing everything up. What has poor old mathematical Spinoza to do with your lyrical gold-beard? You were going to talk about a lap on which you were sitting, do you remember?

Lap. Why are some images so much stornger than others? Why do you associate your hatred of every form of religion and utopia with the utterly unimportant lap of Father Vincent? A lap? It was more like a valley, a valley of brown coarse-haired cloth. My God, how writers can inflate an incident. How many boys at my boarding school haven't sat on the lap of a reverend father and are now themselves vicar general of one or other unpronounceable bishopric in the Philippines, Jesuit in Nicaragua, editor-in-chief of a provincial newspaper in Asturias or plain dead, passed away peacefully? Why am I making all this fuss?

This is why: because I am the only idiot still sitting here at a school desk, and from the size of the desk, the seat of which I have been obliged partly to dismantle in order to fit into it, I can conclude how small I then was. Small and attractive. Thank God I have no mirror in this classroom; otherwise I would be forced to observe that the child of those days has grown into the stout blue-clad person who is sitting here now, perspiring in the heat of forty degrees. Yes, you can check up on it; in the summer of 1989 temperatures of around forty were recorded in Zaragoza!

In spite of my father's anarchist tendencies I was educated at a Carmelite boarding school that has produced several brilliant administrators, first for a bad, and then for a good, government. You can find the school's name in many a biography or necrology. Father Vincent was charged with the supervision of the dormitory, but what he mostly supervised was me and my, in those days, so slender body. And this was not even the worst. He also delivered the Lenten sermons, and I have been susceptible to rhetoric all my life. When he spoke of suffering, hell and damnation, the dark waters of Lethe poured straight from Christ's terrible wounds into the chapel, I drowned in them, in a blend of blood, gall, vinegar and body fluids, a one-and-a-half-meter sinner in short trousers. Worse still, he was my father confessor, which he remained until, for the hundredth time, I shoved the same petty childish sin through the hatch of the confessional as if wanting to wipe it off on his brown habit, and he suddenly hissed at me furiously through the twilit wooden trellis, "you randy buck"; and yet, in the evening, he summoned me out of my bed and pulled me on to his big brown lap again. The coarse cloth rasped against my bare legs, I struggled silently to escape from that valley and those whispers. I didn't want to sit there.

I admit, it is hardly an impressive logical deduction, but ever since that time I have been allergic not only to the laps of Carmelites but, in direct consequence, to the laps of Rome, Moscow, Geneva, Mecca and the Synod of Dordrecht and to the equally smudgy alternatives to those doctrines, to the sects and utopias and to anyone claiming to speak on behalf of something different, something higher and better, and who is therefore lying, to everyone who wants to sit on the lap of a pope or an ayatollah or a Truth and who does not, like me, wish to be alone, merely born and not created, existing on his own like any otter, buzzard or grasshopper.

"Ho ho, Tiburón, old shark, do you really mean that?" my fellow students at the debating club in Delft used to ask when I got carried away. The Dutch always want to know whether you mean what you say. "No, of course not," I would reply. Then they would roar with laughter. "Boys, poor old Tiburón is having one of his days; he's homesick; he's in his Spanish mood." And they made horns of their fingers and sang "Toreador Olé" and filled me up with Dutch gin. But I am still the same. Everyone may think what he likes, and every form of disagreement is permitted, as long as he does not involve anyone else in it. Those who do that, the tempters, I hate, including the insignificant fool who copulates with Lucia while the last golden, then pink, then black, fire glows in the ashes. Yes, of course I can see it. The all-seeing eye of the no one who writes a fairy tale is the most distorted eye that exists; and so it sees also that despite the small distance still separating Kai and Lucia, each of the two lost halves of that perfect pair is living under a different, contrary regime to that which goes by the name of love.

23

O<small>NE</small> morning Kai woke up and knew it had been snowing. He knew it without seeing anything; he heard it because of what he did not hear. Snow muffles; a cloth is spread over the world. He got up and went to the window. The two crows he had observed before were flying in strange curves through the sky as if they were writing. Large flakes fell, covering everything. It is not my country, he thought, and gave a start, because he realized he had not thought anything like this for a long time. He shut his painful eye tightly and the other one halfway, and saw the snow, like a dangerous, glistening carapace covering a silent world to which he was a stranger. The crows settled on the windowsill and became, to his half-shut eye, two black gleaming blurs. He tapped, but they did not go away.

He washed and went outside. In the common room there were, as usual, a few men hanging around whom he did not know, though was never certain of this, for in all those faces one feature seemed to predominate. However much the men belonging to the faces might differ, it

made them resemble each other: an expression of indifference and frozen rage. They seemed, even when Ulrich
was not there, to observe a pecking order unclear to Kai,
which must have been decided by force, as in the animal
world. Force was the element in which they lived; their
movements, looks, voices spoke of force; it was the law
governing their lives. He noticed how some of them scru-
tinized him and was aware of their mockery. The snow
had stirred something in him that had hitherto been dor-
mant. Their voices sounded more agitated than usual.

Just as he was about to go outside, he heard Floris'
voice coming from a side room, and then, harsh and
northern, that of a person he did not know. Kai paused in
order to hear more clearly, but all he gathered was that
someone on whose protection they depended no longer
wished to be involved or was out of circulation and that it
would not be long before . . . and then there followed
whisperings, the whisperings of boys' adventure books
that exist also in real life. Real life?

The voices came nearer and he walked on, out of the
building, into the gardens that led to a wood which was
still part of the enclosed domain. He had walked there
before, but with the snow getting thicker and deeper he
could not easily tell where he was going and soon found
himself in an area he did not recognize. The snow fell on
his clothes and hair, but he scarcely noticed it. A thought
was trying to form in his head, but in his brain it was
snowing too; the only clear thought was that of a white,
icy woman who had driven every other thought out of
him. The wood became deeper, more mysterious. Tall
spruces stood like frozen watchmen on either side of
what must be a path. He was searching for something but
did not know what. After a while he saw behind an ir-

regularly shaped hedge of shrubs a low structure adjoining a high wall. He stood in front of it and stretched out his hand to the door.

It all happened more or less at once: the high-pitched screeching of the geese and the blow that knocked him down. Later he remembered only that when he was lying on the ground, the geese had bitten him everywhere with their vicious hard beaks and that he did not care, because the speck, the splinter, the fragment he had felt in his eye during all that time had vanished with the blow.

24

"I T IS time."

Lucia heard these words very clearly. She saw Anna standing in the tent opening, saw the snowflakes on her shoulders, and looked at the man with the golden beard lying asleep beside her. He smiled in his sleep; he was dreaming of a terror that did not frighten him. He held the keys to the kingdom of heaven; nothing could happen to him. He would not miss his *honyseime*; all women belonged to him, as he belonged to all women. They were one with the essential nature of things—with the unseeable, the divine world—so nothing could ever go wrong.

It did not occur to Lucia to ask what it was time for. Anna, in whose movements there was always something clownlike, as if she constantly raised barricades for herself which she was then unable to surmount, had said it with the same assurance as someone knocking on the dressing room door to announce that it is time to go onstage.

The good thing about fairy tales, thought Anna, who,

according to Andersen's Law, should have exploded at that moment, is that everything, in contrast with real life, is dictated by the outcome. That was why you not only had a simpler character than ordinary people, but why there was also no need to worry yourself about the tedious logic that makes life so difficult for characters in a novel. It spared you much doubt and gloomy reflection. Moreover, as fairy tales always begin with the *idea* of their outcome, they often follow an explosive chronology, and this appealed to her. A situation that might just as well have continued indefinitely is, by virtue of the outcome, interrupted in the most brutal, arbitrary manner: most fairy tales, after all, are no more than a few pages long. That within these closed circuits an entire, independent theory of relativity can arise and, among other things, result in animals and candles being able to speak, may seem strange but isn't. The fairy tale is a province of the realm of the imagination, and everything happens differently there; you might compare it with a pressure cooker. The compression of a large mass of time within such a small span distorts the sound in the animal's mouth (and at extreme temperatures the same happens to the waxen silence of the candle) into that highly differentiated form of quacking, chirping, roaring and bellowing which we in our arrogance call language and which we usually, that is to say, when our narratives are synchronized with our lives, reserve exclusively for ourselves. By the same token, however, it can be argued that the novel has only barely escaped from the talking animals. Anyone who really wants to record the drama of someone's life would have to write a novel as long as life itself. This has proved to be impracticable. Because of the necessary compression that takes place in a novel,

115

people with perfect pitch may observe that the tone of what is said in novels does not usually correspond with reality as we perceive it. If it does, it is often a bad novel. In fairy tales the story is contracted still further, with the result that animals can be heard to speak. The correct formula for the effect of this acceleration is difficult to calculate because you would have to take into account all other characteristics of wolves, mermaids, candles and reindeer. That it has something to do with an intensified process of time is obvious. If the fairy tale characters were given a complex psychology or if they were made to reflect upon themselves, they would probably become totally inaudible or unreadable, as the case may be. This is meant literally, of course.

Therefore, during the whole time that Anna is thinking this, or partly thinking it—since I am here too—and is walking along the snow-covered woodland path with Lucia, she has a splitting headache. Lucia has not; she is cheered by the snow. On this day she was to think three more times of the man who could make love like a cloud and out of whose beard you could wind a hair around your finger like a calendar; and the following week she would think of him twice and after that once every year, without precisely knowing why.

"Are we going to look for Kai now?" she asked Anna, who was busy removing the car from under its plump, double-sized snowy shape.

Anna was about to say, "Today you shall be face to face with him," but she whistled a tune instead. First, the word *today* was without meaning, and second, the whole sentence sounded like something that had been written before.

She wasn't so much surprised at Lucia resuming the

thread so easily, but rather at the number of pages that, at her age, she had had to spend among the lusty crowd. Fairy tale character and at the same time author's accomplice, an impossible position. But she was wise; she was fond of Lucia and liked the exemplary innocence with which the girl had enjoyed her sensuous adventure.

As Lucia's beauty was already perfect, there was nothing to add to it, and yet it seemed as if she had become even more radiant. She danced around the car, crystals of snow sparkling in her hair, and threw the yellow ball, which Anna sometimes thought of as her best friend, high up in the air.

As a surprise, the car started at once.

25

KAI was happy and unhappy at the same time. Un-happy because there is something sinister in the thought that you have been somebody else for a time, happy because this was no longer so.

His hands were tied behind his back; he was lying in a dark shed and had thought of Lucia the whole time. The whole time, that is what we call a small portion which we break off from the real whole time. The thought of her filled him, because she was lacking. It wasn't so much that she was not there—no, she was lacking. His other half, a lovely expression. This book is about reading. He thought of her, but it was to no avail. The other half which is lacking—we are back with Plato again. Writing consists of regrouping what has been written before; there are always a hundred writers hidden in your hand even though you may not know it or wish it. It can't be helped. If you are superior you don't show it; what I do is servant's work.

The expression *other half* is unthinkable without Plato. Kai does not think of that. He feels sorrow, or pain, the pain of loss, the same pain she too is now beginning to feel. But he does not reflect on the pain, he *is* the pain. Can an animal feel grief? No, an animal *is* grief. Not always, but at the moment when we would say that it *feels* grief. A human being feels afraid; an animal is fear. When I say Kai is now thinking about Lucia, I mean that he is, at this moment, the lack of Lucia. Are fairy tale characters the same as animals then? I think they are, and this is why people and animals are of equal value in fairy tales. They can move in only one direction, and reflection is therefore useless. He is the grief that she is not there and he *is* this grief down to every last corner of his body. The grief in his body, his body in a cell, the cell in a castle, the castle surrounded, in total silence, by police, crack troops from the North, where a new government has at last decided to eradicate that hotbed of organized crime in the dark provinces of the South.

All this takes place in a world changed by snow, the same snow through which Lucia now approaches the castle. She has no idea how close she is, nor does it matter; for anyone who has studied the world of fairy tales knows that although place and distance do exist there, the laws governing travel and time are different. As soon as you have said "once upon a time," you have created an extratemporal and extraterritorial reality in which anything is possible. A free-for-all. The characters travel by wild goose or by reindeer. Only the outcome matters.

And the outcome, as I have said before, is fixed. In novels it is different. There, the outcome is still debatable even after it has occurred. That is why, in a novel, the lover can think about Plato. While Lucia walks behind Anna through the snow and Kai tries to fray the ropes that bind him by rubbing them against a sharp stone in his cell, we look at two novels in which this happens. In both, the main character briefly reflects on Plato's *Symposium*. There are now five of us sitting here in my classroom, Plato, Kundera, d'Ors, Andersen and I. Andersen doesn't like me, that is obvious. I break all his rules. I am a denatured writer. It is true; I am. Tomas, in Kundera's *The Unbearable Lightness of Being,* thinks of the famous myth from the *Symposium*: "People were hermaphrodites until God split them in two, and now all the halves wander the world over seeking one another. Love is the longing for the half of ourselves we have lost. Let us suppose that such is the case, that somewhere in the world each of us has a partner who once formed part of our body." To Tomas this is not the woman he is now living with and whom he loves, Tereza. It is someone else, a girl he has dreamed of. What would happen if he found her? Would he then leave Tereza? No, he would not. If he ever were to find the dreamed other half, he would flee from her and stay with the woman who is not the dreamed lost half but for whom he nevertheless feels a love that "he cannot express."

We read Czech writers, but who reads Spanish writers? In *Gualba, She of the Thousand Voices* by Eugenio d'Ors, "the 45-year-old man thinks about Plato's immortal dialogue." "Plato knows about love," thinks the man, "about the search and the tragedy of the search. The myth of the original, unique being—androgynous, later divided into two halves that seek each other in order to be complete together—is full of light. But because Plato was an optimist, he describes the imaginary success of this search, not the ultimate failure. He writes beautifully about the first half of the erotic process but forgets the second half, in which everything goes wrong. Plato is a philosopher and a poet; he is not a lover."

Kundera and d'Ors wrote novels. Plato wrote down a myth that Aristophanes had told during the symposium. Andersen wrote fairy tales. Novels describe how life is because it *can* be so. In a myth an impossible answer is given to unanswerable questions. Something happens there that never happens anywhere. Myths are examples, novels are pictures, fairy tales are beloved lies told by people who find the failed myth of life intolerable. In myths people live forever. In fairy tales they live happily ever after. In novels there is, at the end of the "ever after," the beginning of unhappiness, and usually even before.

In myths everything is solved in some way or other; in novels nothing is ever solved; and in fairy tales the solution is postponed, but if it ever takes place it will be outside the scope of the fairy tale. That is the lie.

I am thinking of the snow in Lucia's hair. I look out over the empty school yard, which consists of a sheet of refracted light—light from which my four friends have detached themselves like shadows—and I wonder where my irresponsible desire to tell lies comes from.

"From unhappiness," says Andersen, who is in a position to know. "But you are not unhappy enough. That's why you can't do it. Lying, too, is an art."

"Why don't you write novels?" asks Kundera. "Then you can lie a reality."

"Reality is only a shadow," says Plato.

"We Spanish have never been very good at dealing with reality," says d'Ors.

"Reality is more in the line of the Dutch," I mutter, but Plato doesn't know who or what the Dutch are, and the other three say nothing.

26

Now the night is clear; it is no longer snowing. Around Orion's Sword the nebula is visible in which new stars are made. Orion is followed by his dogs. There is writing also in the sky. Place the point of the compass in Kai's cell, don't listen to the shouting in the corridors, and draw a small circle. Within it, the policemen are already approaching the castle, pistols drawn; outside it, still in silence, Anna and Lucia walk along a woodland path. Anna advances in a straight line toward the castle, and Lucia, who does not know this, follows her broad figure. She has forgotten the man with the beard; she now exists only as the empty half of Kai, who has to be found because otherwise neither of them can exist. Anna has tied a curious scarf around her head that makes her look like an old reindeer. She doesn't exactly walk; she follows two crows that fly high and far ahead of her, and this makes it look as if she herself is flying, too; every step is a day. The reindeer knows the way; sometimes it rises from the ground, and then Lucia, seated on the animal's back, can see the white world beneath her. It looks as if it is always night, but the night is brighter than the day; the snow reflects the light of the stars. Sometimes Lucia dreams of robbers, of a girl with a knife, of a voice telling her where she can find Kai. Every time she wakes up, the world is still as light as before; she sees the trees standing like soldiers ready for battle; their branches are guns, lances, swords. At daybreak a voice or a trumpet will give the command, and when the trees start to walk, the sound will be terrifying.

The snow crystals hurt her eyes. She is standing on a stage again; Kai must be somewhere in the hall, but this blindfold seems to scorch and blind her eyes; she cannot see him. She feels the presence of all those people; she hears the silence; and then suddenly, as if she were being struck in the face by a catastrophe, the screeching and hissing of geese burst out all around her. They advance from all sides; their necks are straight as sticks, and at the end of each stick is a gaping, screaming beak trying to bite her. Then there are shots. Anna takes off her antlers, and with the hard leather and fur flaps she hits out at the geese's heads until blood pours out of their eyes.

In his cell Kai hears the screaming and shooting and then, closer by, rapid steps in the stone passage and someone turning the lock. It is Ulrich. He cuts the handcuffs and says, "Escape, it's all over here. Don't ever say it was me that let you go. Make sure you're not caught."

"And you?"

"I'll manage."

He pushes Kai into the corridor and disappears. Kai starts walking, hears a northern voice calling, "This way, this way," and the sound of boots. He is sure he does not know this part of the castle but walks away from the sound and the shooting, climbs a winding staircase and

123

arrives in an open gallery with pillars around a square courtyard that he has never seen before. When he is about to cross it, he suddenly sees the Snow Queen. Behind her stands Floris.

"The game is fleeing, Floris," she says in the same voice as always, a voice of glass and ice. Kai sees how Floris takes aim, and he knows he cannot escape and stands still as if for one last time he has been turned into ice; but then he hears a voice saying, unspeakably serenely and, he thinks later, melodiously, "No, no, don't do it," and then he sees a fat old woman whom he has never seen before, and behind her Lucia, stretching out her hand toward him and with her mouth open as if wanting to call out—but then the shot resounds that was meant for him, and the old woman falls, as silently as a large animal, in the snow that slowly turns red.

Another shot resounds, and another, but he does not know who has fired them, for they come from behind, and he sees how Floris, crawling and stumbling, tries to escape while his hands grope at his red throat; but then he also sees the woman opposite him, who is not bleeding and who goes on looking at him as if she were mocking him, scorning him, laughing at him, and who then, with the frozen mask of that laugh on her face, topples forward, breaks, folds, pulverizes, hits the ground, falls sideways and lies in the snow like a broken doll, not far from the other, older woman. Her eyes are open but they no longer see anything. While quick footsteps recede behind him, he goes to her and looks; but as before, nothing can be seen in those eyes except an infinite depth of glass and ice in which anyone who ventured into it would freeze forever. He bends down to close those eyes, and as he does so he sees in one of them a tear like a diamond, hard and cut. He puts his fingers on her eyelids, but they will not close, and he hears a sigh that still sounds like scorn, and the look in her eyes is also one of scorn, but this time it is the scorn of absence. We are *sibbet*, she once said to him, but it was not true. She was never *sibbet* with anyone, and she still looks like herself; he must leave before she gets up. He goes toward Lucia, disengages her hands one by one from the hands of the other dead woman, who sleeps in her bed of blood and snow like a child. The shooting has stopped. He puts his arm around Lucia. Before the boots that are now approaching from all sides have reached the courtyard, the two of them have left soundlessly together. The dead remain behind as if they had always lain there, in the snow that reflects the stars.

27

O F WHAT follows next I can only be ashamed, if for no other reason than my age. Men of my age don't sit in empty classrooms at night. When I had written the last lines, I wriggled with effort out of my seat. Suddenly I had a feeling that the holidays were over, that a rowdy class would enter any minute and find me there as an intruder, as someone who, because of his bones having grown and his flesh having obscenely expanded in all directions, because of the hair sprouting out of his face and of the stink of Ducados, has lost the right to dwell in children's territory and yet wants to dwell there, a trespasser.

They would enter and unmask me as someone already tainted by old age, perhaps already faintly smelling of death, yet nevertheless, perhaps precisely for that reason, wanting to dwell in a world where the tarnished laws of the older generation did not yet apply, where life was not yet a story in which everything tallies, a world in which everything was still to happen and which, because it had not yet happened, could still take any form, because it was not yet, like mine, completed.

126

They would enter rowdily and see me with my too big, closely written exercise book, of no interest to anyone; they would smell the deceit, the lies in me, and suddenly stand in silence; all those bright eyes would look at me with the distaste that the impossible always arouses. They would not even laugh; they would slowly move back and fetch another adult, someone from my own, unalterable world where no one ever comes in and sits by your bed to tell you a story when you ask for one, in which no one suddenly, without any reason, draws a sun with far too big yellow rays, above a mountain smaller than the house beside it.

I whistled, but it did not sound right. Then I looked out and saw what I could have seen all through the summer but hadn't—a hopscotch, one of those chalked patterns of numbered squares joined together, crosswise and then again lengthwise, which I always imagine in some primitive way to represent fate. You complete a circuit and things go well or badly, something like that. Boys didn't play it; at least, I could not remember ever having played it myself. Someone at a university must surely, I thought, have written a study about hopscotch, relating it to initiation rites, kabbala or God knows what. But this did not concern me now, for I felt a ridiculous, uncontrollable urge to play hopscotch. I resisted briefly, but it was three o'clock in the morning and no one could see me in the school playground. I went outside, looked at the squares and realized that I did not know how to play, but I didn't care.

Suddenly I jumped, the way you jump into the sea for the first time in the summer, into the first square, on one foot, and moved with a little skip to the next square. I didn't know what I was doing, but I was happy. The night was clear, the clock struck three and Alfonso Tiburón de Mendoza was playing hopscotch in the school yard. When there were two squares side by side, I jumped in both at once with my legs apart, making one of those elegant little hops I had seen the girls make in the street, and then I continued again on one leg. Where it was supposed to lead I did not know, but I was happy because, while hopping, I had a feeling as if I were still writing the story that lay in the classroom, that ridiculous cuckoo's egg I had laid in the nests of at least ten other birds at once. Only when I was completely out of breath did I stop and sit down on the ground, the way I used to when I was little, when I could still rub my head against the underside of the freestone windowsill. I could no longer do so now, but it didn't matter. The moon had appeared above the roof of the school, and peering at the sky I saw Orion, my favorite star, followed by Sirius, my favorite dog. A patch of white light lay on the harsh square of the playground, briefly creating the impression that it had been snowing, but for the rest there was nothing to be seen.

And I sat there happily ever after.

Let be be finale of seem.
The only emperor is the emperor of ice cream.
—Wallace Stevens

FOR THE BEST IN PAPERBACKS, LOOK FOR THE

In every corner of the world, on every subject under the sun, Penguin represents quality and variety—the very best in publishing today.

For complete information about books available from Penguin—including Pelicans, Puffins, Peregrines, and Penguin Classics—and how to order them, write to us at the appropriate address below. Please note that for copyright reasons the selection of books varies from country to country.

In the United Kingdom: For a complete list of books available from Penguin in the U.K., please write to *Dept E.P., Penguin Books Ltd, Harmondsworth, Middlesex, UB7 0DA.*

In the United States: For a complete list of books available from Penguin in the U.S., please write to *Dept BA, Penguin*, Box 120, Bergenfield, New Jersey 07621-0120.

In Canada: For a complete list of books available from Penguin in Canada, please write to *Penguin Books Ltd, 2801 John Street, Markham, Ontario L3R 1B4.*

In Australia: For a complete list of books available from Penguin in Australia, please write to the *Marketing Department, Penguin Books Ltd, P.O. Box 257, Ringwood, Victoria 3134.*

In New Zealand: For a complete list of books available from Penguin in New Zealand, please write to the *Marketing Department, Penguin Books (NZ) Ltd, Private Bag, Takapuna, Auckland 9.*

In India: For a complete list of books available from Penguin, please write to *Penguin Overseas Ltd, 706 Eros Apartments, 56 Nehru Place, New Delhi, 110019.*

In Holland: For a complete list of books available from Penguin in Holland, please write to *Penguin Books Nederland B.V., Postbus 195, NL-1380AD Weesp, Netherlands.*

In Germany: For a complete list of books available from Penguin, please write to *Penguin Books Ltd, Friedrichstrasse 10-12, D-6000 Frankfurt Main 1, Federal Republic of Germany.*

In Spain: For a complete list of books available from Penguin in Spain, please write to *Longman, Penguin España, Calle San Nicolas 15, E-28013 Madrid, Spain.*

In Japan: For a complete list of books available from Penguin in Japan, please write to *Longman Penguin Japan Co Ltd, Yamaguchi Building, 2-12-9 Kanda Jimbocho, Chiyoda-Ku, Tokyo 101, Japan.*

☐ **A SPORT OF NATURE**
Nadine Gordimer

Hillela, Nadine Gordimer's "sport of nature," is seductive and intuitively gifted at life. Casting herself adrift from her family at seventeen, she lives among political exiles on an East African beach, marries a black revolutionary, and ultimately plays a heroic role in the overthrow of apartheid.
354 pages   ISBN: 0-14-008470-3

☐ **THE COUNTERLIFE**
Philip Roth

By far Philip Roth's most radical work of fiction, *The Counterlife* is a book of conflicting perspectives and points of view about people living out dreams of renewal and escape. Illuminating these lives is the skeptical, enveloping intelligence of the novelist Nathan Zuckerman, who calculates the price and examines the results of his characters' struggles for a change of personal fortune.
372 pages   ISBN: 0-14-009769-4

☐ **THE MONKEY'S WRENCH**
Primo Levi

Through the mesmerizing tales told by two characters—one, a construction worker/philosopher who has built towers and bridges in India and Alaska; the other, a writer/chemist, rigger of words and molecules—Primo Levi celebrates the joys of work and the art of storytelling.
174 pages   ISBN: 0-14-010357-0

☐ **IRONWEED**
William Kennedy

"Riding up the winding road of Saint Agnes Cemetery in the back of the rattling old truck, Francis Phelan became aware that the dead, even more than the living, settled down in neighborhoods." So begins William Kennedy's Pulitzer-Prize winning novel about an ex-ballplayer, part-time gravedigger, and full-time drunk, whose return to the haunts of his youth arouses the ghosts of his past and present.   228 pages   ISBN: 0-14-007020-6

☐ **THE COMEDIANS**
Graham Greene

Set in Haiti under Duvalier's dictatorship, *The Comedians* is a story about the committed and the uncommitted. Actors with no control over their destiny, they play their parts in the foreground; experience love affairs rather than love; have enthusiasms but not faith; and if they die, they die like Mr. Jones, by accident.
288 pages   ISBN: 0-14-002766-1

FOR THE BEST LITERATURE, LOOK FOR THE

☐ **HERZOG**
Saul Bellow

Winner of the National Book Award, *Herzog* is the imaginative and critically acclaimed story of Moses Herzog: joker, moaner, cuckhold, charmer, and truly an Everyman for our time.

342 pages   ISBN: 0-14-007270-5

☐ **FOOLS OF FORTUNE**
William Trevor

The deeply affecting story of two cousins—one English, one Irish—brought together and then torn apart by the tide of Anglo-Irish hatred, *Fools of Fortune* presents a profound symbol of the tragic entanglements of England and Ireland in this century.   *240 pages   ISBN: 0-14-006982-8*

☐ **THE SONGLINES**
Bruce Chatwin

Venturing into the desolate land of Outback Australia—along timeless paths, and among fortune hunters, redneck Australians, racist policemen, and mysterious Aboriginal holy men—Bruce Chatwin discovers a wondrous vision of man's place in the world.   *296 pages   ISBN: 0-14-009429-6*

☐ **THE GUIDE: A NOVEL**
R. K. Narayan

Raju was once India's most corrupt tourist guide; now, after a peasant mistakes him for a holy man, he gradually begins to play the part. His succeeds so well that God himself intervenes to put Raju's new holiness to the test.

220 pages   ISBN: 0-14-009657-4

☐ **THE LAST SONG OF MANUEL SENDERO**
Ariel Dorfman

In an unnamed country, in a time that might be now, the son of Manuel Sendero
refuses to be born, beginning a revolution where generations of the future wait for
a world without victims or oppressors.

464 pages · *ISBN: 0-14-008896-2*

☐ **THE BOOK OF LAUGHTER AND FORGETTING**
Milan Kundera

In this collection of stories and sketches, Kundera addresses themes including sex
and love, poetry and music, sadness and the power of laughter. "*The Book of
Laughter and Forgetting* calls itself a novel," writes John Leonard of *The New
York Times*, "although it is part fairly tale, part literary criticism, part political
tract, part musicology, part autobiography. It can call itself whatever it wants to,
because the whole is genius."

240 pages *ISBN: 0-14-009693-0*

☐ **TIRRA LIRRA BY THE RIVER**
Jessica Anderson

Winner of the Miles Franklin Award, Australia's most prestigious literary prize,
Tirra Lirra by the River is the story of a woman's seventy-year search for the place
where she truly belongs. Nora Porteous's series of escapes takes her from a small
Australia town to the suburbs of Sydney to London, where she seems finally to
become the woman she always wanted to be.

142 pages *ISBN: 0-14-006945-3*

☐ **LOVE UNKNOWN**
A. N. Wilson

In their sweetly wild youth, Monica, Belinda, and Richeldis shared a bachelor-
girl flat and became friends for life. Now, twenty years later, A. N. Wilson charts
the intersecting lives of the three women through the perilous waters of love, mar-
riage, and adultery in this wry and moving modern comedy of manners.

202 pages *ISBN: 0-14-010190-X*

☐ **THE WELL**
Elizabeth Jolley

Against the stark beauty of the Australian farmlands, Elizabeth Jolley portrays an
eccentric, affectionate relationship between the two women—Hester, a lonely
spinster, and Katherine, a young orphan. Their pleasant, satisfyingly simple life
is nearly perfect until a dark stranger invades their world in a most horrifying way.

176 pages *ISBN: 0-14-008901-2*